FICTIONAL FATALITY

A SHELF INDULGENCE NOVELLA

S.E. BABIN

OLIVERHEBERBOOKS

WANT TO KEEP UP WITH NEW RELEASES?

You can grab a FREE set of stories here if you sign up for my newsletter.

Or, you can click the kitty cat and follow Sheryl online at sebabin.com. She emails only when she has a new release or has messed something up. And even then she sometimes forgets...

ONE

I peered down at Poppy through the metal crate door of her carrier. We'd just left a vet visit, and from the show my cat had put on, you'd think she'd wound up alone in a minefield. I'd never met a more dramatic cat than the one currently hissing beside me.

"Calm down, Poppy. It's over. And you're welcome you won't ever get heartworms, you ungrateful feline."

Poppy yowled.

I snorted and kept walking, weaving in and out of tourists on the sidewalks. The vet was only a couple of blocks away, so I'd walked her over there today because of how busy the traffic was. If I'd driven her, I probably wouldn't have gotten a spot. I'd given Poppy a fuzzy blanket and draped one over her carrier before whisking her back out the door and down the street to my shop.

The air outside was brisk and the weather gloomy. It was a typical winter's day in Silverwood Hollow, cold enough to freeze your nose off and dreary. I'd bundled up in a puffer jacket, a knitted hat and a massive scarf wound up almost to my nose. My hands were gloved, and I wore waterproof boots. There were few things worse than getting water in your shoes when it was below twenty outside.

New Year's Eve was almost upon us. Christmas decor still twinkled everywhere and the town still had a festive, hopeful air to it. I felt grateful for it and for the peaceful lull in my life, especially after a couple of weeks ago when I'd solved the murder of a local author.

If I never solved anything again, it would be too soon for me.

The crowd ahead of me grew even thicker. Poppy stilled in her carrier and finally settled down, much to my relief. I stepped off the curb to get around several people milling on the sidewalk. Traffic was blocked in the main area of the town square during the holidays, forcing vehicles to go around if they needed to get out of town. It was a hassle, but I'd lived here long enough to get used to it by now. Using my own car would have been more hassle than it was worth.

I stayed off the sidewalk and milled in between chatting families and couples. Just as I was about to cross the street to get to my bookshop, Tattered Pages, a shout of alarm slowed my footsteps.

Poppy shuffled in the carrier, and I turned to see a middle-aged man swaying in the middle of the square, his hand over his heart. A woman stood next to him, her expression frantic. His mouth opened and closed like a fish out of water before his knees collapsed under him and he slumped to the ground.

My heart pounded in my chest. I rushed over to the poor woman and set Poppy's carrier down. "Ma'am? I'm Dakota Adair." I pulled out my cell phone. "I'm going to call 911, okay?"

The woman turned unseeing eyes to me. I reached over and squeezed her arm.

When the dispatcher answered, I rattled off what happened and where I was.

"Is he breathing?"

"Hold on." I set the phone down and touched two fingers to the side of his neck.

Nothing.

I moved my fingers around, desperately trying to find a pulse.

Nothing.

The woman, presumably his wife, began to whimper.

"No," I answered.

The dispatcher asked me if I knew CPR.

Poppy took that moment to start yowling her head off. I listened as carefully as I could, handed my phone over to a stranger next to me and began chest compressions to the tune of *Staying Alive*, all the while praying it wasn't too late.

The woman next to me quietly sobbed. I tuned her out the best I could, tuned out the noise and whispers swirling around us as I worked.

The next thing I remembered was a strong hand squeezing my shoulder.

"Dakota."

I continued to compress and blew breath into his lungs. *Ah. Ah. Ah.* The voice sounded like it was underwater.

"Dakota."

The voice sounded familiar. Someone crouched down beside me. "Hey."

I turned to him, my hands never stopping. "Hardy?" My voice cracked.

His eyes filled with sympathy. "It's okay to stop."

I shook my head. "No."

"Dakota. He's gone."

A breath slipped from me. "No," I said again.

Hardy took my hands. Another officer escorted the sobbing woman away. Noise came back in then, a loud whooshing sound through my ears. He gripped my freezing hands in his own and pulled them close. "Look at me."

I took a shaky inhale and met his concerned blue eyes. His brow furrowed as he stared at me. "It's okay. You did what you could."

I shook my head. "I should keep going."

Hardy shook his head. "Come on." He tugged my hand and helped me stand, then steered me away from the poor man.

Dozens of people stood around, staring at me with wide eyes.

"Make a hole!" Hardy barked. Everyone moved, and it looked like water, opening up a passage for us to walk.

"Poppy," I said after a moment.

"One of my officers has her." He pulled me closer against him and I let him lead me, my thoughts numb.

"Hey, Brody." Hardy jerked his head at someone. Moments later, a tall, handsome man stood in front of me.

"Hi, Miss Dakota. Mind coming with me for a second?"

I blinked up at him. His eyes were so brown. "Where?"

"I think you might be suffering from shock. I'd like to examine you."

I shook my head. "I don't think so."

Hardy gripped my elbow. "Please. It will only take a moment."

A sigh escaped me. I peered up at him. He didn't look angry or annoyed or anything but concerned. I relented. Normally, when something like this happened and I found myself in the middle of it, Hardy was hopping mad. Today he just looked worried.

"Five minutes," I told Brody. He gave me a relieved smile and took me over to the back of the ambulance parked a few feet away. I didn't even notice it had arrived. Glancing back over my shoulder, people still milled around, but the police were slowly moving them behind barriers.

Brody helped me into the back of the ambulance. "What do you think happened?" I asked as I sat down on the hard bed.

"From what everyone told us, I have to guess a heart attack." Brody shook his head. "Scary how fast those can happen."

I shut my eyes for a moment. "That poor woman."

Brody turned back to me, holding a blood pressure cuff. "She's lucky she had you."

"Is she?" I snorted in derision. "I couldn't help him."

Brody gave me a long look. "But at least you were there to try." His gaze flicked over to the gawkers and I could see the disgust on his face. Not much brought out curiosity like a death or a crash. "That's more than the rest of them standing there can say."

I fell silent and waited while Brody examined me. A few minutes later, he nodded. "I want you to go straight home and rest. And you should take tomorrow off."

He was lucky the shop was closed anyway. I had a full four glorious days off thanks to how the holidays fell. "Okay."

Brody blinked. "Just like that?"

He sounded so shocked I had to laugh. "My shop is closed for the next two days."

"Well, lucky for both of us then. When I tell people to take it easy, I usually get the look." He chuckled. "We work too much in this country."

"I agree," I murmured. We sat there for a moment in silence until I slid off the bed. "Thanks for checking me out, Brody."

"Any time, Miss Dakota. Be sure to let Detective Cavanaugh know you're okay."

"If I see him. He's probably going to stay busy for a while." He helped me out of the ambulance. I looked around and saw a young, unfamiliar officer holding Poppy's carrier. She must be freezing. I hurried over to her and took it from him. "Thank you," I breathed.

"Any time, ma'am."

He stood next to the man's body. I swallowed hard and tried to look away. When he fell, he'd dropped a book. It still lay beside him, the pages fluttering in the wind. I swallowed hard and edged around him, hoping to make a wide berth. Poppy screeched, startling me out of my thoughts.

I pulled the side of the blanket up to check on her. She stared at me with those chartreuse eyes. Just as I was about to drop the blanket, she yowled again. I shook my head and started to walk again, but Poppy screeched and hissed. I sat the carrier down and crouched to peer in. "Poppy. You are being so rude! Do you have any idea of what kind of day I've had?"

Poppy turned her head and peered through the slats of her carrier, even though the blankets were still there. I frowned and pulled up the side of the blanket until I could fully see her and find out what she was yelling about.

Her gaze landed on the man's outstretched hand. Just on the edge of his fingertips rested a book. A familiar one. My heartbeat thudded in my chest. I took a quick, furtive look around. The officer's attention was on the crowd, so I scooted a little closer and peered down. The pages fluttered in the wind, but I recognized the spine and cover. This came from my store, from my collectible case.

Harper must have sold him something while I was at the appointment with Poppy. I started to walk away, only for Poppy to hiss at me. Frowning at her sassy attitude, I glanced once more at the book only to see a small slip of paper in between some of the pages. A slight gust of wind came, and the paper curled and blew a few feet away. I glanced down at my cat, who stared up at me with too wise eyes, and quickly walked over and scooped the slip up before anyone was the wiser.

Tugging the blanket back down over the carrier, I hurried away from the crowd and back to Tattered Pages. As soon as I walked in, I set the carrier down and breathed a great sigh of relief as I unlatched the crate. Poppy shot out of the crate and disappeared into the romance section.

Harper stood at the register ringing up a young woman holding a baby. Readers would find a way no matter what. With a baby in the house, I wondered how and when she found the time. Considering I couldn't be trusted to go to sleep at a normal hour when I had a good book in hand, this new mom must be exhausted.

I gave her a bright smile after I let Poppy out of the carrier and nudged my head toward the office for Harper to know I needed to speak to her. Her forehead crinkled, but she nodded.

I tugged my jacket off, hung it up, snagged a cup of coffee at the stand we'd set up, and headed into my office.

Another day. Another murder.

Welcome to Silverwood Hollow, I guess.

TWO

The paper in my hand felt cold and soggy. I tossed it on the desk in front of me, stared at it for a moment, and took a few sips of coffee to settle my nerves. I'd never performed CPR before and had never been involved in a medical emergency of that magnitude. Everything inside of me felt like jelly, and if I were home, I probably would have fallen face-first onto my bed and slept for a week.

As it was, we'd been super busy these last couple of weeks, and I only had Harper on board with me. Adding another employee had occurred to me several times, but I wasn't ready yet. In a business like this, ebbs and flows between busy times and slow times were natural, and I would have hated hiring someone only to cut their hours again.

Harper was happy with the extra hours, and I'd just given her an additional raise after the Mary Ruth disaster.

Trust me when I say she deserved it. I tried not to speak ill of the departed, but Mary Ruth had been a nightmare. To just about everyone she encountered.

Harper had just bought a house and found herself stunned by all the extra costs involved. I'd been that way too when I first bought this property. It seemed like every single tiny thing ended up draining your savings and that was just before you moved in.

I chewed on my lip and eyed the paper in front of me. Why was I worrying about this? It was obvious the poor man died of a heart attack. I snatched the paper up, unfolded it, and chewed on my lip as I recognized the familiar name and number.

My name and number.

HARPER STEPPED into the office a few minutes later. The uncurled paper still lay in front of me. It didn't mean anything. Lots of people had my name and number. After all, I did own a bookstore in a popular tourist area. But few people had my cell phone and that was the number scrawled underneath my name.

I held up the paper when Harper took a seat in front of me. Her hands shook as she crossed them on her lap.

"I just heard," she said quietly. "I'm so sorry that happened."

"I think it was a heart attack. Or something like that. It all happened so fast."

Harper's brow furrowed. "What is that?"

"Poppy alerted me to the book he had. It came from our store. This fell out of it."

My assistant frowned. "We've been really busy today. What did he look like?"

I rattled off his description and watched as her eyes widened.

"He came in maybe thirty minutes before you got back." She paused. "I think he wanted the signed Hemingway, but we sold that one a few weeks ago."

I remembered. I hadn't wanted to sell it, but I never wanted to sell any of my books. A bad habit for a bookstore owner, for sure. It was a first edition, signed copy of *Death in the Afternoon*. When Harper told me someone came in asking about it, I'd gotten the shakes. The book was worth close to five grand and I wouldn't let him touch it without gloves.

Sometimes we had people come in who weren't serious about rare books. They just wanted to handle them just to say they had. This man seemed different. I remembered him as quiet and intense, soft spoken, and knowledgeable about what he was buying. It was the first time I'd ever felt so good about a sale. I knew it was going to a collector and not a reseller. I did the best I could to prevent selling anything to someone I knew would turn right around and sell it again, but I couldn't weed them all out. This man had the look of someone who'd grown up around books and cherished them as much as I did.

"That's strange," I murmured.

Harper caught on right away. "That two people would

come in asking about the same obscure book?" She nodded. "I agree. But I don't understand why he would have your cell phone. Who knew we had the Hemingway?"

I thought about it. I didn't list all of our books on our website, especially not the rare ones. I was always afraid of break-ins. Granted, Silverwood Hollow didn't have a lot of crime, but there sure had been a lot of murders around here lately, so I couldn't be too careful. "I can't think of anyone local," I admitted. I'd just gotten the book in a few weeks ago from an eBay auction. I scored a lot of good deals like this, mostly from sellers who just wanted to get rid of things, or estate sales from children unequipped to deal with all the belongings their parents had left behind. Sometimes they didn't even care what something was worth as long as there was someone willing to take it off their hands.

I'd gotten the book for way cheaper than I expected and listed it through a third party service. I never used my real name or the shop name when I listed books through it, so if someone messaged me to see it, I usually declined. People could buy the book directly through the site and that's what I preferred. The owners vetted every single seller, so fakes were few and far between. This meant they knew who I was even as the browsers did not. The thought made me very uncomfortable, especially given that I'd used my cell phone number.

"Just Raptor Books," I said thoughtfully.

Harper blinked. "They have all your info."

I nodded. "But this book wasn't worth more than a few thousand."

Harper and I locked eyes. "Are you sure?" she asked.

"I usually double and triple check everything." My mind spun as I tried to remember. We sat there in silence for a moment before I snapped my fingers. "I did. I remember it. It was a first edition. Valuable, but not obscenely expensive. Not for a first edition."

Harper's look turned thoughtful. "What did Hardy say?"

I'd fled the scene before Hardy could say anything. I cringed internally. He shouldn't be too upset about this one. I didn't do anything except be there when it happened, and I'd tried to save him. "Nothing. On the surface, this looks like a medical emergency. Nothing more."

Harper eyed me. "Buuuuut?" she drawled.

My lips twitched. I didn't want to get involved. "But, it sure is strange for two people to be looking for the same book in my shop that I didn't list in town."

Harper stood and grinned at me. "I'll leave you alone while you call Hardy."

A groan slipped from me. "You want to do it?"

"Nope!" she wiggled her fingers in a wave and slipped out the door.

THREE

Hardy and I were in a strange little dance. One day, I thought he liked me. The next, I wondered if he wanted to strangle me. On another, I'd catch him looking at me with a strange expression on his face, one I couldn't decipher. I knew how annoyed he got with me every time I managed to get caught up in a murder, but I couldn't help myself. I think he knew that, too.

Hardy couldn't say I was ineffective. I'd been anything but. I might be a thorn in his side, but I'd helped with his cases more often than not. Sometimes I wondered if it was a combination of me putting myself in danger and getting into Hardy's business that made him hold himself back from me. But then there were other days where I wondered if I wasn't a gazelle being hunted by a lion.

I dialed his number by heart and waited for him to answer, my heart pounding in my chest.

"Dakota," Hardy said, his voice warm and concerned.

My face heated. "Hardy."

"You okay? Brody said you hightailed it out of there."

"I'm okay. It was too cold out for Poppy and she was already grumpy. She had a vet appointment today."

"When is she not grumpy?"

I laughed. "You aren't wrong there. Sorry I didn't stick around."

"It's not a problem, but I'll probably stop by the shop later with some more questions. Are you free around four?"

"I am."

There was an awkward pause. "Hardy. Something flew out of the book that man had."

A long sigh came over the line.

"Don't be like that! It had my name and cell phone number on it."

"The book was from your store, wasn't it? He had a receipt in his bag."

"Well, yes," I said. "But -"

"No buts. The man had a heart attack, Dakota. There was nothing strange about his death." I could hear the barely concealed growl in his voice.

"He came in today looking for a rare book."

"You *do* have a bookstore," Hardy drawled, sounding unimpressed.

I huffed a breath. "I'm aware. But the weird thing is, someone else came in a few weeks ago asking about the same book."

"I'm still not sure where you're going with this."

"If you let me finish, I'll tell you!" I protested.

Hardy's low chuckle came through the line. "I'm all ears."

"Thank you. This book wasn't online. Only on one site. No one in town knew I had it. I listed it on the site, but I never used my real information. The only people who knew I had the book were the owners of the site."

"And you think the two are connected?"

"As much as I don't want to, yes, I do. No one knew I had that book and for two people to come in relatively close together asking about it seems strange. Plus, only a few people have my cell phone number in town and none of them are in the book trade. The only other people in the trade who have it are Harriet from Binders and the owners of Raptor Books."

"It seems like a reach," Hardy said.

I sighed. "Fine. I just wanted to let you know."

"Now wait a minute," Hardy said. "I didn't say I wasn't going to check it out."

I blinked. "Really?"

Hardy huffed a laugh. "Is it that far-fetched?"

"Well, yes!"

"This doesn't mean I want you involved in the case. In fact, consider this a warning to stay out of it. We don't think there's foul play, but we'll follow up on this tip because the victim was relatively young to have a heart attack or stroke."

"Thank you," I said, mollified.

"You're welcome."

I opened my mouth to say goodbye, but Hardy interrupted me. "And Dakota?"

"Yes?"

"Stay out of it. I'm serious this time."

My mouth snapped shut. I didn't even say goodbye this time when I disconnected.

Goodness. Save me from a bossy man.

I STEPPED in to relieve Harper a little while later. She shot me a grateful glance and as soon as she finished ringing up her last customer, she grabbed her cardigan and waved.

"I have a carpenter coming over to the house in just a little while." A stand of long blonde hair fell over her eye as she bent down to get her bag. "I'm having bookshelves installed."

"Ooh, jealous," I said as I switched out the cash drawers. "What color?"

She shrugged. "I'm either going to go neutral, like a dove grey, or I'm going to go weird. Super weird. Like navy. Or maybe even bright orange."

My brows lifted at that. "Orange?"

She snorted. "Okay. Maybe not orange, but it would look really good if I painted the walls navy."

I tried hard to imagine it and couldn't. "Orange might be hard to match with accessories. If it's a bookshelf, you may want to read close to it right? Is there a window?"

"You need to come by the house," she cajoled. "We've both been so busy that it slipped my mind. How about dinner next week?"

"That sounds great, actually. I'd love to see the house." I grinned at her. "And try to talk you out of the orange shelves."

"Navy walls, burgundy chairs?" she asked as she slid her sweater on and shouldered her handbag.

I clutched my chest. "Dear god, no."

She snorted. "See you in a couple of days!"

And that was the moment I remembered Harper scheduled time off. I peeked outside. Dozens of people milled around, their arms full of shopping bags.

I really needed to hire some more help.

FOUR

The slip of paper stayed in my mind for the rest of the day. Just as I was about to lock up, a tall man came around the corner and waved at me from outside. I blinked, stunned to see Everett Adams.

My heart did a strange flip flop in my chest and I pulled the door open. "Everett. Hi!"

I'd first run into him, literally, at a coffee shop in the next town over, when I was trying to investigate Mary Ruth's untimely death. He was a lot of things: handsome, intelligent, funny, and successful. He'd also coined the name the "book slinging sleuth." Which I hated, by the way.

I hadn't seen him since Mary Ruth's case ended, so I was surprised to see him now.

"Dakota! I'm so glad I caught you." He winced as he saw the time. "I know you're closing, but I got so behind today. I wanted to see if you were interested in any of our selections."

My eyebrows rose. Everett was an acquiring editor at a mystery imprint. "You're here about books?"

He blinked. "Um, yes. Is that okay?"

I motioned for him to come in. "As long as you brought a sleeping bag and some energy drinks!"

His amused chuckle rolled over me as he stepped inside. I looked at the large leather bag he held with anticipation.

"Do you want some tea?" I asked as I locked the door behind us and flipped the lights back on.

"That sounds great. Is over here okay?" He headed over to the small seating area I'd set up. Two older chairs and a small wooden table were tucked close to the women's fiction area.

"Sure. Are you hungry?"

Everett turned those honey brown eyes to me. "I am, but I don't want to keep you too long. I feel terrible that you were closing up."

"This is about books. You can keep me forever and I won't mind."

At his raised eyebrow, I colored a little and cleared my throat. "You know what I mean."

The twitch of his lips said otherwise. "I'd love dinner. What about delivery? I don't come to Silverwood too often, so I only know of a few restaurants."

I thought of Sprinkle Heaven, but she only had sandwiches and smaller fare. "Do you like Italian?"

"It's my favorite, actually."

"There's a great place down the road. I'll check to see if they deliver. Usually I make pasta at home, but since you've brought me new books, I can splurge tonight." I poured both of us a cup of tea from the still hot kettle and brought it over. He took it and settled into the seat. Everett wasn't a small man, and his knees looked a little awkward as he sat in the smaller chair.

"Hold on." I set my cup down and rushed back into the office. I dragged out a larger wingback chair and motioned for him to get up. "Try this one. It's much better."

Everett sat down. Relief passed over his face. "Thanks. It's the curse of height. I rarely fit into regular chairs."

"No problem." I motioned to his bag. "Let's order first and then you can show me the goods."

He laughed as I pulled up the menu for Giovanni's. Ten minutes later, we realized we both had the same taste for Italian food and two chicken and mushroom crepe orders were on the way.

Everett opened his bag and pulled out no less than ten books. I leaned forward eagerly.

"Harriet isn't too happy with me that I'm visiting you first."

I blinked and looked up at him. "From Binders?" I narrowed my eyes at him. "Considering I just met you a little while ago and had no idea that you even brought books to bookstores, I'd say you're the one falling down on the job?" I kept my tone easy and joking, but Everett blushed.

"Caught," he said and huffed a laugh. "To be honest, Candlelight Springs kept me pretty busy. I've been meaning to get over here, but I'm still relatively new to the area." He dipped his head and waved his hand in a mock bow. "I hope you can forgive me."

"It depends on what you brought me."

He spread the books out, and I quickly perused the titles. He had a few cozies, a couple of historical mysteries, and two thrillers. The other ones looked like women's fiction.

"Anything paranormal?" I asked, thinking of the new elderly ladies' book club that just started. They all had a weakness for a hunky paranormal detective and a sassy sleuth.

He dug in his bag again and pulled out a few more. One of them had a garden scene with a magical cat, the other was a witch paranormal, and the last one had a diner scene. "Hmm. How does this work exactly?"

Everett rattled off the information and I sat back and listened. I didn't have any direct relationships with anyone who held a position like he did, but I did like seeing novels before they were released. I agreed with his terms and he produced a contract. Just then, someone knocked on the door.

I looked up and breathed a sigh of relief. The food was here. Everett scrabbled for his wallet, but I held my hand up. "My treat."

I unlocked the door and handed the guy a tip. He handed over a paper bag that smelled mouthwatering. "Be careful out there!" I called. The weather was still positively frigid, but the end of the long winter was near.

After locking the door back, I headed back over to Everett who'd cleaned off the table. The books were stacked neatly by his chair. I handed him over his food and some utensils. "Give me a second. I have soft drinks in the back and a bottle of wine. You like white? It would go well with this."

"I sure do," he said. "Thank you."

"Sure." I got up and headed to the back kitchen. Harper and I didn't stock a lot in the back because we both lived so close, but we did stock the fridge with drinks on a regular basis. I dug through the back and found a nice bottle of white. Just as I was about to pop the cork, I stilled.

I peered over my shoulder at Everett. His dark, messy hair rested against the collar of his Henley shirt. He wore a dark pair of jeans and a nice pair of shiny leather shoes. Had this turned into...

I blinked. This wasn't a date, was it? I turned and frowned down at the wine. Shaking my head, I took out the cork and poured us two glasses. No. This was merely two peers working and bonding over books.

I settled myself with a deep breath and headed back out with the wine. Everett, to his credit, waited for me before eating. "I hope you like this place. It's one of my favorites."

"It smells divine," he said.

"Dig in then but toss me those books before you get too distracted." I grinned at him and took a sip of wine.

We spent the next hour eating and hammering out a schedule of when he would come by again. The publishing business was one I never could wrap my head around. He never knew how many books he'd have on his calendar at any given time and when he got a good manuscript, he told me it could take up to a couple of years to publish it.

"Imagine all those good books we haven't read yet," I said and sighed.

"So true," he agreed. "I have at least a hundred waiting for me in my inbox right now."

My eyebrows rose, but he held up a hand. "But not all of them are good. In fact, most of them won't be. I'm searching for diamonds, but I'm also searching for the rough stones too. The ones I can polish and make amazing."

"It sounds like an awesome job."

He nodded. "It really is." Everett stood and stretched. "Thanks so much for letting me in and for the dinner." He nudged the pile of books with the toe of his shoe. "You can keep those."

Delight filled me. "Really?"

"Just don't put them on the shelves. There's a disclaimer on the front cover. These are all advanced reader copies and not for sale."

"Don't worry. I'll hoard them for my own collection."

Everett gathered his coat and shrugged it on. "Good. I'll see you again next month. If not sooner."

"Let me grab the keys for you." I rushed over and unlocked the door for him.

He waved as he headed out into the night and I watched his lean back as he disappeared into the shadows of the town.

Disturbed, I shut the door and locked it, wondering what this was and why I felt so weird about it. Hardy's handsome face intruded into my mind and I shut it out right away. I wouldn't feel guilty about having dinner with a peer. I was an unattached woman. This was the way it worked.

But the odd feeling didn't leave me for the rest of the night.

FIVE

I opened the shop ten minutes early the next morning just because I had everything finished early and I was itching to get busy. Today was Sunday and it was a coin toss as to how busy the square would be today. Some Sundays I had to hang on for dear life. Others were slow and easy. I hoped for a slower day because I had some research to do.

Hardy usually wouldn't give me any information on victims, but since he thought this one was natural causes, I wondered if the media would have listed his name. I debated calling Cole, but we were in an odd sort of limbo after the last case we worked together. Granted, he'd saved me and Mom and Corky, but I hadn't seen him after that.

We used to have a standing lunch date, but he hadn't called me for quite a while. Swallowing my pride, I decided not to call him. I'd head over to his work during my lunch break to see if he was still there first. Cole was known to burn the midnight oil.

"Poppy?" I called. She'd kept herself hidden since the vet visit. No surprise there. The cat hated those visits with a fiery passion and would ensure I knew it for days to come. It didn't matter why I took her either. Grooming, a nail clipping, or something as simple as a checkup. No matter what it was, she came home with a grudge.

Normally she poked her head out when we had a new visitor, but I hadn't seen her since I'd taken her out of the crate. She'd been coming home with me more and more, but I wouldn't be surprised if she elected to stay here tonight and the next. I hadn't been able to find her last night either, though I did hear her rustling around in the back before I'd left.

I poked around for a few minutes calling her name, but there was no sign of her. Shrugging, I headed into the kitchen to make sure she had food and water. She didn't come out even with the rattle of the food bag, but I put a little extra food in there just as an apology.

When I came back out, the bell over the door rang and a harried looking man came in, scowling at the umbrella he held. He shook it outside and tucked it under his arm after he closed it. He was short, slightly taller than me, and had a receding hairline and a bulbous nose.

"Welcome to Tattered Pages. May I help you?"

The man's dark eyes found me. "Yes. Are you Dakota Adair?"

I stilled. "I am. Why?"

He scurried forward and pulled his bag over his shoulder. "My name is Montgomery Ambrose. I represent Holland Clark."

I stared at him. He looked at me expectantly like I was supposed to know who that was. "Okay," I said after the silence turned awkward.

"Holland Clark," he said again.

"I'm sorry, Mr. Ambrose. I have no idea who that is."

His expression cleared. "Ah. My apologies. Holland Clark is the man you..." he coughed. "Assisted the other day."

My brows drew together. "Assisted?"

"Yes. The man who collapsed yesterday. You called authorities and performed CPR."

"Oh." I swayed and leaned against the register. "Oh. I'm so sorry. Is his wife okay?"

Mr. Ambrose's expression cleared with relief. "As well as can be expected, my dear. They'd been married for twenty years."

"So awful. Please pass my condolences on to her if you don't mind."

He gave me a strange look. "I certainly will."

"Can I help you find something?"

The man cleared his throat. "You have no idea why I'm here, do you?"

I slowly shook my head. "No idea. Are you looking for a book?"

Mr. Ambrose laughed, and it sounded dusty and disused. "No, I'm afraid not. I'm here on Mrs. Clark's behalf, actually. And his as well." He looked around the store. "Am I the only one here?"

"You are." I poured him a cup of chai tea and handed it to him. "Fresh and organic. Would you like to have a seat?"

Relief spread over his features. "I'd love that."

"This way." I led him to the same area where I'd had dinner with Everett last night. "Please have a seat."

Mr. Ambrose situated himself and pulled out a leather briefcase. I watched as he unsnapped the buckles and pulled out a sheath of papers. "I hear you have a knack for solving crimes the police have trouble with."

I blinked at him as a slow understanding of why he was here hit me. "I occasionally get lucky," I said slowly. "But this is not without me putting myself into some serious danger." The last case replayed in my mind and I swallowed hard, trying to blink back tears. It hadn't only been me in danger that time. My family had gotten involved and any taste I had for sleuthing was beaten back when they'd gotten involved. If I ever helped anyone again, I would be way more careful never to involve them in it.

"My client feels that her husband did not die of a heart attack like the authorities claim he did. She's seeking to prove he was the victim of a targeted attack."

I let out a deep exhale. "I'm sorry, Mr. Ambrose..."

He kept speaking, his gaze on me. "Furthermore, Mrs. Clark seeks to hire you to prove this fact and is prepared to offer you a generous fee for your findings."

"I'm not a private investigator," I argued.

"Mrs. Clark is aware of your occupation. However,

after this misfortunate occurrence, at least two people in your town came up to her with tales of both your heroics and your sleuthing skills."

I wanted my chair to swallow me whole. "There were no real heroics involved. I got lucky most of the time and my sleuthing 'skills' are really just earning people's trust."

"Exactly," Mr. Ambrose said. "You get people to talk to you when others can't or won't. I wouldn't call what you've done luck exactly. I did some digging myself. I support Mrs. Clark in this."

"And if I fail?" I asked.

"You won't be paid." He shrugged and pushed a sheath of papers across the table. "Nothing more to it than that. You'll find her offer more than generous."

I didn't pick it up. "I'm not sure I'm comfortable with this. I don't earn pay for what I've done. I've done it because it was the right thing to do."

"And because your friends or your business was involved. I understand. But Mr. Clark was a stranger. No one you know was involved with him. Consider this a transaction, Ms. Adair."

At my look, he leaned forward, his eyes pleading. "You don't know me, but Mr. Clark was a good man. A personal friend of mine. His wife and children are grieving. I don't mean to impress upon your guilt, but well, I find myself in a position where I must. The police plan to mark his death as natural causes and we both feel like there's more to it than just that." He straightened. "Also, Mrs. Clark wishes to thank you for trying to save her husband. Few people would do what you did."

He stood. "Please, take a look at the contract. I think you'll find it's fair and more than generous."

I nodded, still too stunned to speak.

"And Ms. Adair, I think your skills may be far more suited to sleuthing than books. Perhaps there is a way you can do both, though?"

He didn't wait for me to respond before he headed out the door.

I sat back in my chair, my breath whooshing out of me.

SIX

Right after I locked up, I headed over to Cole's work still reeling about the offer Mr. Ambrose presented to me. I hadn't dared open up and look through the papers yet. I'd brought them with me. Cole was used to perusing documents and looking for anything strange. Maybe he could help me.

I still felt a little angry at him, but after he'd come into my store and saved us all, it was hard to stay mad at him. Our friendship was broken, yes, but I didn't think it was beyond repair. The door was open, so I breezed in. Since it was after dark, the receptionist had already gone home, leaving me free to head into Cole's area.

"Cole?" I called out as I headed into the dim interior. Several cubicles were set up, but everyone had gone home. I walked further in and headed over to his office, peering around the door.

Cole sat in his desk chair, his posture slumped, staring at his computer screen. He hadn't heard me come in. I debated knocking, but instead quietly cleared my throat so as not to scare him too much.

"Cole?" I questioned when he didn't hear me.

He inhaled sharply and spun to me, his green eyes wide. "Dakota! You scared me."

"Sorry." I held my hands up, the papers in my left. "I'm here for some help if you have a minute."

His gaze turned curious, and he flicked a hand at me. "Sure. Have a seat."

Remembering the last time I'd asked him for help made an uncomfortable feeling twist in my stomach. "I wondered if you might take a look at these for me and see if there's anything off about them?"

Cole's brow crinkled, but he pulled the papers toward him. Silence fell, but a moment later, his eyebrows went up and his bright green gaze flickered up to me. His lips twitched. "Do you know what this is?"

My shoulders slumped. "Someone wants to hire me to investigate a murder."

He snorted and sat back in his chair, one foot crossed over his knee. "Someone paid attention and finally paid you what you're worth."

"I can't take money for this. It seems... wrong."

Cole shook his head. "So the entire field of private investigation is wrong? Or police officers? Or detectives? Or -"

I laughed. "Okay! I get it. But they're all highly trained."

"I don't think it matters." He tapped the paper with his index finger. "Leave this with me and I'll finish looking over it and I'll have a lawyer friend of mine look at it too. I don't see anything alarming with it, but I'm a journalist, not a contract lawyer. Can I get this back to you in the morning?" His brow furrowed all of a sudden and his gaze drifted back to the contract. When he looked back up at me, there was a gleam in his eye.

"I thought he died of natural causes." Cole's eyes were beginning to go blank as they normally did when he was on to something. It was like he disappeared into his head and everything else got left behind.

I shrugged. "His wife doesn't think so."

"The last time we did this, something happened between us." Cole's voice lowered.

"I think it was more of a combo of a lot of things," I admitted. "Not just this."

He swallowed and looked down. "I miss you."

Tears swam in my eyes. "I miss you too."

"I'm still a journalist, Dakota."

"I'm aware. But are you my friend, too?"

Cole blinked and stood up in one quick motion. Before I knew it, he'd reached down and engulfed me in a warm hug. I inhaled the fresh scent of him and put my arms around his waist.

"Always," he said against my hair. "I am *always* your friend."

I sniffed against his shirt. "Thank you for saving me. And Mom and Corky."

"I truly have no idea how one family can find so much trouble," he muttered before kissing me on top of the head and letting go.

I missed the warmth of him, but the uncomfortable feeling in my stomach had disappeared. We were okay.

Finally.

I DROVE HOME FEELING BETTER than I had in weeks. Cole said he'd come by as soon as he could in the morning to look over the paperwork the lawyer had left. A large part of me had no desire to take someone else's money for something like what happened to Mr. Clark, but I also didn't want to get tangled up in another investigation. However, I already felt that intangible pull I always felt when I was being led down a darker road. I couldn't help myself.

There were things about this that weren't adding up, so I felt inclined to agree with Mrs. Clark. A heart attack was a convenient way to go and would cover up a lot of sins if someone didn't know to look deeper. And there were a lot of ways to cause a heart attack. Poison. Anger. Stress. Certain drugs. Happiness. Though I highly doubted Mr. Clark died happy.

I had to agree with Hardy. On the surface, this looked tragic but normal. But two people coming in looking for an obscure, valuable book in my shop made the coincidence look like something more sinister. I tapped the steering wheel as I drove home thinking about where to start with this. I'd take a deeper look at the contract once I got it back from Cole. I hadn't even looked at it yet, so I didn't know how much money they were offering.

The bookshop was doing well, but there were some improvements I wanted to make over the next year or two. Plus, I wouldn't mind eventually purchasing a newer house with a larger property. I had never added that to my list simply because I never thought I would make enough money to do both. But Silverwood Hollow and my shop along with it were beginning to blossom into something more.

I FOUND I missed Poppy's yowling when I was at home alone. She was only quiet when she wanted to be and most days, she didn't want to be. I tossed my keys on the hall table, kicked off my shoes, and headed straight to the back to put on my pajamas. The sun set so early this time of the year that even if I got home at six p.m., it still felt like the middle of the night.

Once I got comfortable, I poured myself a glass of red wine and fired up my desktop computer. I pulled up a search engine and typed in the name of the Hemingway book I'd sold. I didn't expect to find anything about the one I'd sold, but I typed in the information anyway and scrolled through the results.

As far as I could tell, my hunch had been right. The man I'd sold it to was a collector and didn't put it back up for sale. Different versions of the book were all over the place, though, so I clicked a few times to look at the value and the condition of some of them.

It wasn't until I was just about to click off when my eye caught something on a collector's forum. I sipped my wine and scrolled down a post when I froze.

Bookmadness104 had written he'd heard about a first edition book with hidden jewels inside of it. At first, the horror of destroying a first edition book welled up inside of me until I realized how perfect of a hiding place it was. Especially if any jewels were worth well over the price of the first edition.

I scrolled down further to see many people dismissing it outright and calling it an urban legend. A few people wondered about the validity but conceded it was possible. Most of them had no idea where the book was until a post dated a few weeks before I'd sold the book, calling attention to my post on Raptor.

I clicked on Bookmadness104's profile and sent them a message.

Hi! My name is Dakota Adair. I own Tattered Pages, a used bookstore in Silverwood Hollow. I used to be the owner of the edition you spoke about here, but recently sold it to someone else. Can you tell me more about the supposed hidden jewels?

I signed my name and sent the message, thinking it

would be ignored as a lot of things were in cyberspace. A quick glance at the clock made me blanch, so I took another sip of my wine and went to brush my teeth.

I had the day off tomorrow and didn't want to waste it sleeping in.

*

SEVEN

prinkle Heaven smelled exactly like its namesake. I opened the door, inhaling the strong coffee, cinnamon scent and felt my shoulders drop at least two inches. Trudy, the owner and one of my good friends, waved at me, her face split wide in a grin.

"Hey, honey!" she called, motioning me over. "Come see what we have today."

I groaned. Trudy knew these were the magical words that would ensure I walked out of here loaded down with baked goods and a few extra pounds on the hips. "I'm not sure if my heart can take it," I said as I dutifully headed over to the register.

She stood there with one of her younger helpers, a young girl with stick straight blonde hair whose name I couldn't remember. I smiled at her even as I glanced down to look at what marvelous concoction Trudy had come up with this time.

It wasn't even ten in the morning and I found myself looking at an enormous ... something. "A brownie?" I guessed.

"Mm hmm," Trudy said. "But more than that. This is a stuffed brownie."

I blinked. "Stuffed?" I had to laugh. "You are positively diabolical."

She grinned at me. "I haven't named it yet, but it's a stuffed rocky road marshmallow fluff brownie." She reached over for a squeeze bottle and poured a generous helping of what looked like caramel all over the top. "With a freshly made sea salt caramel sauce."

I squeezed my eyes shut. "You've outdone yourself."

She pushed the brownie over to me. "Try it."

I almost whimpered. I hadn't even had coffee yet. But who could resist such gooey goodness? "Did you make the fluff yourself?" I grinned at Trudy's horrified expression and laughed out loud as she swatted me with her potholder.

"Dakota Adair! You almost offended me with that question. Nothing comes out of my kitchen from a jar."

"I know that. I just wonder sometimes if you should slow down and let the young'uns catch up to you."

"The second I do that is the second I hang up my apron," she grumped. "Now eat."

I obliged and took the fork she handed me. I cut into the brownie, only for marshmallow fluff and pecans to squeeze out between the brownie. Scraping up a little caramel with it, I took a bite.

Flavor exploded in my mouth. She'd toasted the marshmallow before she'd put it in the brownie. How in the world had she done that without burning it? There were hints of smoke and fluff, roasted pecans, the salty sweet flavor of the caramel, and the deep, sultry taste of chocolate. Along with ...

"Is that chili, Trudy?"

She nodded. "Is it too much?"

I slowly shook my head. "It took me by surprise, sure, but it adds something to this. A depth I've never tasted before." I took another bite. "This is hands down my favorite creation. How did you know my weakness was marshmallow?"

Trudy grinned knowingly. Who was I kidding? Anything in Trudy's shop was my weakness. Not just marshmallow. "Ring me up for this and a large coffee, if you don't mind."

"That isn't for sale yet. It's on the house since you were my guinea pig." She nodded to her helper. "Annie, go grab her a large coffee and be sure to leave her some room for creamer, okay?"

The girl scampered off.

"How's the expansion going?" I asked. Recently, she'd opened up a second location and the investors expressed interest in a third. They were all outside of Silverwood Hollow, one in Candlelight Spring's, much to Harriet's delight, and the other about 45 minutes away in a town I'd never heard of.

Trudy leaned against the counter. "Stressful." She

rolled her eyes. "Mainly because it's hard to let go of my baby. I want to have my fingers in everything and I'm learning that's the fastest way to lose my mind." She reached over and patted my arm. "Enough about me. Tell me about you." Her voice lowered. "I heard about that man who died. Such a shame." Trudy's eyes turned sympathetic. "But darling, you're the talk of the town. Don't you be surprised when handsome, eligible men start knocking on your door after what you did for that poor man."

The thought horrified me. "I did what anyone would have done."

Trudy slowly shook her head. "No. You didn't. From what I heard, not a single person stepped up. We all think we're a good person until something like this happens. That's when the people who are truly good step up. It's not a matter of brains. It's a matter of courage and heart. And you have both." Her smile turned downward. "And, honey, that's you. Don't try to diminish it."

My throat clogged with tears.

"If Hardy doesn't see what he's letting slip through his fingers, well. I guess he deserves what's coming to him."

My eyes narrowed at her even through my tears. "Spill," I demanded, my voice thick with unshed tears.

"Word on the street is you had a pasta date." Her eyes glittered with mischief.

"How in the world..." My voice trailed off. This was Silverwood Hollow. The Silverwood Silverettes struck again.

Trudy laughed at my expression. "No one is safe from those adorable little blue hairs."

"They're not adorable," I grumbled.

"So tell me. How did the date go?"

Trudy's assistant finally brought my coffee over and set it in front of me. "It wasn't a date. He works in publishing and had a bunch of books he wanted to sell."

Trudy huffed. "How many of those do you have a pasta date with?"

I glared at Trudy, but she only laughed. "I was hungry and he came after hours. I offered him dinner. We had some contract stuff to work out, so we ate together. It wasn't a big deal."

"I wonder if Hardy knows." Trudy's look lingered.

"I am a single woman and Hardy hasn't given much indication he'd like to change that." I sounded salty about that, but I couldn't help it. I waved a hand. "I don't want to talk about Hardy anymore. Or Everett." Or anyone involving my love life or lack thereof. She hadn't said anything about Mr. Clark, so I assumed no one yet knew that the family suspected foul play. Could I be one step ahead of those Silverettes?

Trudy took my plate and fork and put it on the silver tray of other dishes waiting to be taken to the back. "If you ask me, that man is a fool."

"Trudy," I groaned.

She chuckled. "Fine. Fine. I get it. No Hardy talk. Or date talk. I just want to see you happy, you know?"

I nodded. "I know." Adjusting my purse over my shoulder, I ordered a couple of chocolate chip cookies for the road. Trudy handed them over and I reached around the register and gave her a hug. "You're as bad as the Silverettes," I murmured.

She waved me away. "How can I not be? You're the most fun we've had around here in years!"

And wasn't that a scary thing?

EIGHT

Cole waited outside Tattered Pages. I wasn't working today, but I wanted to stop in and check on Poppy. She was being awfully quiet since I found Mr. Clark. Cole straightened as I got closer, unfolding his long, lean body to his full height. He was dressed casually today in a faded pair of jeans, a royal blue sweater that made his green eyes slightly darker, and a pair of old brown boots. His blonde hair was messier than usual. He looked relaxed, much better than he'd been lately.

He waved the envelope with my contract. "Got a second?"

"Sure do." I unlocked the door and Cole held it open for me. "Come on in."

Cole followed behind me and headed back to my office. I frowned after him and hurried to lock the door so I could catch up.

Cole had already spread out on the small couch I had in the office when I came in. He grinned lazily at me and waved the folder around.

"Sit," he commanded.

I tilted my head. "I am not a dog, Cole."

He laughed. "I bear wonderful news. So, please. Sit."

I pulled a chair over and sat a few feet away from him. "Nothing weird in there I should be aware of? No firstborn children clauses?"

Cole sat up and handed the envelope over to me. "I don't know how you manage it, but this is a well written and fair contract." He shook his head. "There's not a single thing in here to trick you."

I chewed on my lip. "Really?"

Cole stared. "You never looked at it, did you?"

I shrugged. "It didn't seem too important. I wasn't thinking about taking the job."

He snatched the envelope back from me. "Hey!" I called, yanking my hand back.

Cole pulled the sheath of papers out and flipped through them, stopping at a page and shoving it over to me. He pointed at a highlighted area of the contract. "Look."

I frowned at him but looked down at the sheet of paper. I blinked. My eyes swam. Slowly I lifted my eyes back to Cole.

He nodded. "Yup. And that's exactly the reason why you should take it. Swallow your pride and help this woman find out what happened to her husband. Consider yourself a private investigator for a few weeks." Cole sighed and leaned back. "If I were you, I'd strongly consider opening up a firm. I looked up salaries for private investigators. They aren't bad. You'd have to get a license for it, but the requirements aren't too bad."

I swallowed hard, still staring at that number. "I'm a bookseller."

"Who says you can't be both? You have the knack for it." Cole reached over and rummaged through my chocolate stack.

"I'll think about it."

"Don't think about this one. Even if you decide to never do this again, that's a payment I wouldn't pass up. Think of all the things you could do around here. Or for yourself."

I hugged the contract to my chest. "Thanks, Cole."

"Sure thing." He popped a Hershey kiss into his mouth. "Any plans for today?"

"I'm trying to track down the owners of Raptor Books."

Cole sat up straight, interest sparking in his green eyes. "Really?"

"Yes." When I didn't say anything else, Cole snorted and tossed a kiss at me.

"For Mr. Clark?" he pried.

"Yes."

"Can I come with you?" His eyes were hopeful.

"You can."

He lit up and fist pumped the air.

I held up a finger. "If you know this is off the record. We can talk about some of the information you can use, but Cole, you can't do what you did to me last time." My tone had turned serious. "I don't think our friendship could survive it."

He placed a hand against his heart. "Off the record, I promise. But, you agree to give me something. Right?"

"I will. Seriously, though, you get all the good scoops these days anyway, so does it matter?"

Cole rolled his eyes. "How can I stay on top if I don't stay in your good grace?" He grinned at me. "Sign that. Right now. Read over it first, but neither I nor my friend saw anything wrong with it. The worst that will happen is if you don't solve it, you won't get any money besides expenses."

I gaped. "They'll pay expenses even if I don't solve it?"

Cole stood and winked at me. "And that isn't all. You'd be crazy not to sign it." He leaned against the wall and crossed his arms. "Do it. I'll wait."

My stomach wasn't quite the same after I signed the document and scanned a copy over to Mrs. Clark's lawyer. The fee they offered me was more than I made in an entire year working in my shop. Granted, I didn't pay myself much of a salary and hadn't for a couple of years now, but that was about to change with all the new business I'd gained. This was the first year I'd been a little more than comfortable and the feeling gnawed at me. If I solved this murder, I'd pull my salary and enough to put a nice down payment on a house and have enough left over to expand the store.

Mr. Clark, whoever he was, had been a very wealthy

man. Cole rode beside me, a quiet and comforting presence. It was nice to know he hadn't judged me for signing the contract and, in fact, had encouraged me to do it. I wasn't sure how Hardy would feel about it, so I planned to keep quiet about it until it undoubtedly came up. He found out everything no matter how hard I tried to keep it from him.

"Have you ever been to Merlin Hollow?" I asked Cole.

"It sounds like something out of Harry Potter," he murmured. "The news has never taken me there. This is an adventure for me just as it is for you. Though I hear there are feral cats all over the place." He grimaced.

"Funny," I murmured even as I tried to imagine it.

"I'm serious."

I chanced a quick glance over at him and blinked. He wasn't kidding. "Oh my. They're running through the streets?" I shuddered.

"It's like Virginia's version of cat island." Cole shivered. "Remind me again why we're going there?"

I burst out laughing. "You have to be kidding me. Where's their animal control?"

Cole's lips twitched. "I swear to you. I am not lying. It's what they're known for." At my look, he shrugged. "I don't get it either."

I looked down at my pants. "I'm wearing black."

"Ooh," Cole teased. "That's kitty kryptonite."

Forty minutes later, we took the street into Merlin Hollow. The tree cover was much heavier here. Long, heavy oak boughs formed a canopy as we drove down the main road. We traveled for a few minutes before I chanced a look over at Cole.

His brows were drawn together as he scanned the woods on either side of us.

"Not a single cat."

"Yet," Cole intoned in a foreboding voice.

I rolled my eyes and kept driving. My GPS told me to take a right and when I turned onto the street, three cats darted in front of my car. I screeched on the brakes.

"What in the world," I whispered.

"Cat island," Cole said grimly. "It's like the lost boys, but with cats."

I huffed a laugh. "Coincidence," I said, but I couldn't shake the odd feeling. "There's no way a civilized town would let itself get overrun with cats."

"Maybe the mayor is elderly and single."

"Wrong. Wrong. Wrong." I chuckled. "You're going to have to apologize to the mayor when you see her."

He turned wide eyes to me. "We aren't going to see the mayor."

When I stayed silent, he stared at me. "Are we?"

"Depends," I said. "You never know how a trip with me will go."

Cole groaned. "That's what I'm afraid of."

We took a few more turns until Raptor Books loomed ahead of us. The company had a massive warehouse behind it. In front of it was a cute little building with a painted red door and a cute window display full of books. I loved a window display as much as the next shop owner, but I didn't let any books stay in there for more than a day. Sunlight damaged books easily, and I valued all of my stock.

A lot of people didn't feel like I did about it, but I cringed every time I saw a book in a window, especially if I detected even a hint of fading. We parked and headed up to the front door, Cole a comforting presence behind me.

I tried the door, but it was locked, so I rang the small bell on the wall. A few moments later, the door opened and a small blonde woman peered at us.

"Can I help you?" She had light brown eyes, elfin features, and was casually dressed in jeans and converse, with a long-sleeved shirt pushed up to her elbows.

"Yes, my name is Dakota Adair. I own Tattered Pages. It's a bookstore about forty-five minutes away." From the research I'd done, Raptor was owned by a husband and wife team. There were no pictures on their website, besides all the books, but the woman's name was Catherine Rappaport. Her husband was named James.

"Are you by any chance Catherine?" I asked.

Her eyes narrowed. "Who's asking?"

I paused. "Um. Me. Dakota Adair."

Behind me, Cole coughed to cover a laugh.

"Hold on." The woman slammed the door.

I let out a laugh.

"I thought all bookstore owners were smart," Cole murmured.

"Maybe she's just having a bad day," I offered.

"Dakota, always so charitable."

We stopped talking when the door opened again. This time a man stood there. He loomed over me and Cole, so he had to top six foot three at least. "Can I help you?" the man asked.

"Yes, I'm Dakota Adair. I'm here because I think there might have been an information leak. I'd like to speak to the people who own Raptor if possible."

The man eyed me, his dark gaze flicking down to my shoes and up. I resisted the urge to squirm under his perusal. "That's impossible," he said.

"What is? An information leak or me talking to the people who own this place?" Was I on Who's on First? I seriously felt like I was being pranked.

Cole coughed again.

"Raptor Books has never had a single information leak in all the time it's been open."

"Uh huh. Well, I listed a book on your site a few weeks ago. I invited one of the individuals to my shop through communication through your website, but the second person who showed up for the book should not have known I had it."

"Then you must have told someone else," the man said with a sniff.

"The only person I told was you, Mr.?" I raised my eyebrows while I waited for him to give me his name.

His eyes narrowed. I didn't like the way he looked at me. "Rappaport," he finally bit out.

"Very nice to meet you," I said pleasantly. "When I use your site, I only use your site. I don't even offer the book on my own site or keep it out for public perusal. I've had a great track record of sales, despite the high commission you take on it." I bared my teeth in a sharp smile. "Though I agreed to the high commission when I listed with you, I expect some things to happen when a company takes a cut that big. Do you know what the main thing is?"

The man blinked at me a few times.

"Security," I said when he didn't answer. "And safety."

Cole hadn't said a word, just stood behind me. His steady presence strengthened me. "I'd like to talk to you about this. It's cold and you haven't welcomed us in and I'm probably one of your better customers."

He wordlessly held the door open. I looked back at Cole. His eyebrows rose, his green eyes glittering with wicked mischief. I turned and walked into Raptor Books with Cole close at my heels.

James led us down a relatively dark hallway and back into an office that had the distinct scent of moldy books. I shouldn't have been surprised by this, especially after his treatment of us at the door, but my stomach sank. Thankfully I didn't have to send my books to them to list. They merely acted as the middleman and got my book out to collectors. Their reach was wider than mine, but the way this guy ran his ship, my mind spun with the future implications and ideas of how I could improve it.

Maybe I could talk to Harriet after I left here.

The blonde woman came in, her face a mask of anger. "Would you like some refreshments?" she bit out.

Cole put on what I liked to call his charmer smile. "Thank you so much, Miss..."

She blinked at him and her anger slowly melted away. It *was* hard to stay angry at someone as good looking as Cole. "Rappaport," she said.

The man cleared his throat. "Mrs." he bit out. "My wife, Catherine."

The woman stood abruptly, Cole's spell broken.

"I'd love a cup of tea if you have any," Cole said.

Catherine glanced over at me, her eyes glittering with dislike. "Nothing for me," I said. I was thirsty, but I wasn't thirsty enough to risk being poisoned and from the look she gave me, I thought that might be a distinct possibility.

She left us with her husband. He'd settled in behind his desk. Behind him loomed a massive credenza stuffed to the gills with books both new and old. To the right hung several photographs of him and Catherine and two sullen children - a girl and a boy. "You have a lovely family," I lied. If they were anything like these two were, I bet their family dinners were *very* awkward.

"Let's cut to the chase, Ms. Adair," he said. "What exactly are you accusing us of?"

"I've already accused you," I said sweetly. "What I'm looking for now is information."

"You have no proof," James said. He leaned back in his chair. A self-satisfied smile slid onto his face.

Cole finally spoke. "Do you know who I am?"

James frowned. "Should I?"

Cole spread his hands out. "Perhaps my feelings

should be hurt, but I'm willing to overlook it. My name is Shelton Margraves. I'm a reporter for the New York Times."

I stiffened in my chair but made no other move. My expression went blank as I stared at Cole wondering where in the world he was going with this.

James' grin slid from his face.

"We're investigating some corruption in the rare book industry. Unfortunately your name came up more than once. My colleague here might own a small shop, but she is quite well versed in the comings and goings of collectors and shops in this world. If she says she thinks your site released her information, I'm inclined to believe her." Cole pulled out a pen and a small notepad from his shirt pocket and clicked the pen. "How do you respond?"

James blustered. "I am not consenting to be inter-viewed! You came here under false pretenses!"

I held my hand up in a placating gesture. "Mr. Rappa-port. We can keep this off the record, I'm sure." I slid my gaze over to Cole. "Can't we, *Shelton*?"

Cole shrugged. "It's up to you, I suppose."

"I'd like to know who you gave my information to and why?"

James turned as red as a tomato. "I didn't give it to anyone!"

Cole clicked his pen again and wrote something on his notepad.

James looked at it and back at Cole. His forehead broke into a cold sweat. "I - I - didn't do anything!"

Catherine walked back in with a cup of hot tea for Cole. "Oh relax, James." She set the tea down with a click. "I did it."

Guilt slid across James' features.

I wasn't in the least bit surprised. "Who did you give it to?"

She shrugged and sat in a seat next to her husband. "Some guy named Rick. He said the book was stolen and that he needed to get it back."

"But why?" I shook my head. "Surely you've had people say things like this before. Why would you give out my private info now?"

Catherine laughed, a harsh, sad sound. "Do you think it's easy making money in books?" she hissed. "We're barely making do. James over here is obsessed with books. The spines. The covers. The words." She rolled her eyes. "Meanwhile, we've had beans and rice three nights in a row."

I gaped at her. "But what about all the commissions you're making?"

She snorted at that. "Someone got a little big for their britches and got us into a mortgage we can't afford." She jerked her thumb behind her. "And that warehouse you see back there? Cost us a bundle and we've barely got a tenth of it occupied."

"So he paid you," Cole said, his eyes gleaming. "How much?"

"More than my worthless husband makes on this site in a year," she said, malice dripping from her voice.

James stared at his wife, stunned, hurt written all over his features. "Catherine."

She held up a hand. "Don't. I listened to you for years talking about how we were going to be *rich*. Do you call this rich?" Catherine snorted and rolled her eyes. "We're dying out here, James." She stood. "I expect you'll see yourself out?"

"Can you tell me anything else about Rick?" I asked her. The urge to leave overwhelmed me. The conversation James and Catherine were about to have was something I had no desire to witness.

"Don't know much. He was tall, heavy set. Dark hair." She looked up in thought. "He had a scar next to his left eye shaped like a crescent moon. Odd guy." With that, she left the room, leaving me, Cole, and a distraught James.

I rose. "I'll be going now."

Cole stood beside me. I didn't take a step out for a moment. My heart hurt for James. Secondary was the thought that I would never, ever use their site in my entire life. But, that also made an opening for me.

Cole put a hand under my elbow and steered me out. Before I left, I blurted out, "I'm so sorry, Mr. Rappaport."

He blinked but didn't say anything. I walked out of Raptor Books feeling like I'd just flown in like a hurricane and destroyed the place.

NINE

Cole and I were silent for a while on the way back. I'd given him the keys, and he'd taken them silently, deftly navigating us through the streets. We saw five more cats before we left that town in our rearview, hopefully forever.

"That was one of the saddest things I've ever seen," Cole said.

"It sure was, Shelton Margraves." I shook my head. "What in the world were you thinking?"

Cole grinned. "It got him talking, didn't it?"

"Sure did. And probably got him divorced, too."

"We can't help everyone, Dakota. He would have found out eventually. And you never know. He might be complicit and just a good actor."

I didn't think he was. The grief on James' face seemed genuine. "That poor man," I murmured.

But Cole was on to other things. "This Rick guy. Who do you think he is?"

"No idea. But a crescent moon scar... People would remember that. I may ask around."

"I've never seen anyone with one," he mused. "But I'll ask too. Silverwood Hollow gets a lot of visitor traffic these days, so maybe someone has spotted him."

"I don't know how that links to Mr. Clark."

"Well, they were both asking about it. Rick just didn't come to you. So how did Mr. Clark find out?"

"That's a good question. Is it possible Rick is the killer?"

Cole grunted. "Too big of a leap. We don't have anything linking Mr. Clark to any of them."

"We need to find out what was so special about that book." I always inspected the spine, cover, and flipped through the pages looking for damage, but I didn't recall seeing anything interesting about it.

Cole's face turned thoughtful. "What if," he mused, "something was hidden inside the books?"

I'd forgotten to mention the jewels. I told him about what I found, but Cole frowned. "Jewels? It seems too difficult to hide those in a book."

I agreed with him. "Why would they say it then?"

"Maybe it has something to do with jewels," he mused.

"What do you mean?"

"Maybe someone left something in their will to someone. Maybe it's a document. That would be a lot easier to hide, wouldn't it?"

I nodded, chewing it over. "Much easier. I flipped through the book, though, but didn't find anything."

"Everything was normal about the book?" he asked, his eyes on the road. The surrounding trees were mostly stripped bare by the winter, giving the area an odd skeletal appearance. The tree limbs swooped high and low, their dark wood stark in the gloomy sky.

"I think so. I didn't find anything odd about it. The collector who bought it didn't say anything about it either."

"They wouldn't," he said, sounding so sure I looked at him.

"He inspected it while I sat right there."

"Are you sure?" Cole questioned. "What did he do exactly?"

I thought back. "He opened it, flipped through the pages..." My voice trailed off. "Well, I'll be darned." That's all he did. Then he wrote a handsome check. "Do you think the buyer knew?"

Cole grinned. "I'm going to guess yes. He must have gotten there first and whoever really wanted it, maybe Rick, couldn't handle it."

"It still doesn't explain Mr. Clark," I said.

"Nope, but we have several leads now," Cole said. "We'll figure it out."

I glanced over at him. *We.* I liked the sound of that.

I dropped Cole off at his house and headed right to the shop to check up on Poppy. When I unlocked the door, she sat a few feet away from the door staring up at me.

"There you are!" I opened her crate, and she walked in, her tail high and haughty. I shut the door and picked her up, remembering at the last minute to lock the shop doors.

I tucked her safely into the back and drove back to my house.

When we got inside, I let her out and wandered to the kitchen to shake some food out for her.

She sniffed, scarfed it down, and watched me as I made a quick salad. "I'm glad you're home. You're kind of a strange cat, you know that? I've never seen one as antisocial as you. Aren't you scared to be by yourself in a dark store like that?"

She blinked chartreuse eyes up at me. "It would scare me. I can barely be home with the lights off."

Poppy meowed and walked away, having had enough people time for the day, I guess.

I poured myself a glass of red wine and took the salad to the kitchen table where my laptop waited. I fired the computer up and started searching for jewels and rare books. A couple of Reddit threads popped up about the darn book I used to have, but it didn't shed any light on anything for me.

Then I started searching jewels and Virginia. That went about the way I thought it would for a while. Not well. I searched diamonds and rubies and every gem I could think of until I stumbled across something called mineral lights.

My heartbeat picked up a little at that and I leaned forward to peer at my computer. I'd never heard of mineral rights, but apparently it was an important thing to look for when purchasing a property. If you didn't have them and suddenly found oil or silver or a number of other things on your property, the person who owned them could claim them. That seemed a little egregious to me, so I kept digging.

It suddenly hit me. What if the book held information about mineral rights somewhere and not necessarily jewels?

I glanced at the clock. It was still relatively early. Hardy might still be at his office. I picked up my cell and dialed.

"Dakota?"

His deep voice sent chills down my spine. "Mineral rights. What do you know about them?"

Hardy's low chuckle made me smile. "I'm always surprised when you call me. You never know what it's going to be."

"What are they exactly?"

"My understanding of them is basically anything under ground. Oil, silver, gemstones, natural gas. All those things are covered under them."

"I think this has something to do with that book I sold. The one Mr. Clark was looking for."

Hardy sighed. "Dakota."

Annoyance reared its ugly head. "You never trust me until I have to hit you over the head with something. "

Silence fell over the line. Hardy huffed a breath. "You know what?"

"What?" I snapped.

"You're right."

I sat up straight. "What?"

He laughed, a genuine, loud guffaw. A silly grin spread over my face at the sound of it. "I'm going to listen to you this time. Where are you?"

"At home."

"Mind if I come by?"

I swallowed hard. "Uh. All I had was salad for dinner. Are you hungry?"

"I'll grab something on the way."

"No. I insist. I'll whip up something for both of us. I'm still hungry."

"If you're sure," he said. "I'm about to leave the office."

"I'm sure," I said, feeling butterflies fluttering all over. "Poppy is here so be careful not to let her out."

"I'll watch for her. See you in a bit."

We hung up and I stared at the phone like it had bitten me. "What just happened?" I murmured to myself. Moments later, I sprung up and rummaged through the fridge while I tried to find something easy but filling to make. I rarely ate salad because I was still hungry before I even finished with it, but I also wanted to watch what I ate.

I closed the fridge and went to the pantry where I pulled out a pack of gnocchi. I checked the date just to make sure it was still good. Then I went back to the fridge and pulled out a bottle of sun-dried tomatoes in oil, spinach, garlic, and heavy cream. From the spice cabinet I pulled Italian seasoning, salt, pepper, garlic and basil.

Twenty minutes later, I had a pan full of soft, pillowy gnocchi in a rich sun-dried tomato sauce and a pile of garlic bread on the stove. The doorbell rang shortly after, and I pulled off my apron, fluffed my hair, and opened the door.

Hardy stood there wearing a pair of slacks and a blue long sleeved shirt rolled up to the elbows exposing tanned, muscular forearms.

"Hey," I said, feeling all gooey.

"Hey." He held out a bottle of wine. I took it and let him in. Poppy didn't try to run out the door. She just sat there and stared at Hardy before she meowed loudly. He reached down and scratched her behind the ears, then took a seat at the kitchen island. "That smells amazing."

"It's gnocchi."

His brow furrowed. "What?"

"It's a potato pasta. It's soft and pillowy, but I fry it a little to crisp it up. It's one of my favorite meals."

"I can't wait to try it." His bright blue eyes focused on me and I felt my knees weaken. I turned.

"I'll get you a plate. Want some garlic bread?"

"I sure do." His voice rolled like honey over my skin.

I shook my head and tried to put the sound of his voice far, far away from me. Hardy was the most eligible bachelor in town. And yet he was here with me. Aggravating Dakota. The woman who wouldn't stay out of his cases. I thought at one time he liked me. Then it sort of fizzled.

Then it happened again, and I got all excited again. And once again, it fizzled.

This time, I swore I wouldn't get all soft and gooey inside. Hardy could have any woman he wanted. I was the thorn in his side he couldn't get rid of. Why would he want me?

I dished him up a generous helping of the gnocchi and added two of the slices of garlic bread to his plate before dishing up some of my own. He opened the wine he brought and poured us both a glass.

We fell silent while we ate, though I chanced a glimpse to see if he liked it.

With his first bite, his eyes widened in surprise, and he immediately took another bite. I hoped he liked it. Aunt Corky showed me that recipe. She was a lot of things, but the woman had a secret talent for dishing out some amazing meals.

"This is amazing," he said after a swallow of his garlic bread.

"Thanks. It's a great comfort food meal."

"I can see why you like it. I'll have to get the recipe from you."

I looked at him. "Or I can just make it for you again."

His eyes flared in surprise. "Or... you can do that."

I shrugged. "If you want."

Our gazes met. "I want," he said.

I ducked my head before he could see my cheeks burning crimson.

"So, tell me about the mineral rights."

I hesitated, but then dove into my theory. He asked several questions and we ate and drank wine while we talked it out.

When dinner was over, he sat back and tilted his head up to the ceiling. "It sounds far fetched."

"But plausible?" I asked hopefully.

"Maybe. But there aren't a lot of places around here that have a lot of minerals. Most of them are already mines."

"Maybe something was discovered recently and just kept well hidden."

"See what else you can find out. I'll make a note in his file."

I blinked. "Wait. You actually want me to investigate something?"

Hardy grinned. "Like I could ever stop you."

I couldn't help myself. I sprang from my seat and threw my arms around him. Hardy rocked back on his seat but caught me around the waist. Immediately, I regretted my impulsive gesture, but when I tried to pull away, he held me tight. Our eyes met, our noses almost touching.

"Dakota."

I blinked and swallowed hard, my heart pounding so hard I thought it might gallop out of my chest. "Yes."

"We should go out. Together. On a date."

"A date?" I echoed.

"A date," he repeated. "You. Me. I pay. You demur. I insist. You pretend you want the salad. I encourage you to get the pasta. So you settle for the chicken. Even though I know you really want the pasta. I get the steak because I'm manly. You excuse yourself to the bathroom so you can text Trudy and tell her how handsome I look. I pretend not to notice. We eat. We talk. I drive you home." He paused. "I kiss you goodnight."

"You do?"

He nodded.

"And then what?" I asked breathlessly.

"And then we do it again."

"Kiss?"

"Yes. And then go out."

"Again?" My limbs felt heavy and weak. I was firmly under his spell. This was the most he'd ever talked since I first met him and all I could hope was he kept saying these wonderful things to me.

"Rinse and repeat."

"I -" I loosed a breath.

"Say yes, Dakota," he growled.

"Yes."

"Thank God," he muttered. A moment later, he leaned forward and brushed his lips against mine in a tender kiss.

We stood that way for a moment before he finally let go. "Friday?" He stood and took his plate to the sink to rinse it off.

I nodded, numb.

He turned back and I nodded again, not sure I could speak.

"Bring a jacket, a hat, and gloves. We'll be outside." Hardy headed toward the door. "Don't change your mind."

I would never, ever, change my mind.

Hardy grinned at me and left me standing there in the kitchen, completely dumbstruck.

TEN

Murder was the furthest thing from my mind when I woke up the next morning.

I had a date. With Hardy. Handsome Hardy. The man I'd been thinking about since I'd first met him. And he'd asked me out. He was interested in *me*.

A sloppy, goofy smile struck me. I stared up at the ceiling, my thoughts a gooey mess for at least five minutes before Poppy yowled indignantly for her breakfast.

I groaned and rolled out of bed. Heaven save me from a grumpy cat.

She sat in front of her food bowl, an accusatory look on her face.

"Forgive me, Queen Sheba. I had other things on my mind." I poured her a bowl of food and gave her some fresh water. Then I bowed to her. "There you are, your highness."

She stuck her tail up and brushed past me to her food bowl.

I headed straight to the coffee pot. I could tell no one about this date. It would blow through the town like wildfire if I did. People would find out soon enough. Unless Hardy was very careful. Part of me imagined he would be. Maybe we could keep it a secret for a while. I rolled my eyes at that. Avoiding the Silverettes was darn near impossible, but we could try.

I shoved my mug under the nozzle and popped a biodegradable k-cup into the slot. Moments later, the heavenly scent of java rose through the air. I was trying to take my coffee black these days, though every taste was a grimace. Working next to Trudy had made me more conscious of my sugar consumption, and I figured I was more tempted by her store than my kitchen, so I tried to refrain from using sugar at home because I knew she'd have something delicious there.

I took a sip and winced, but it was hot, and it was caffeine. Little else mattered other than that. I padded over to my laptop and fired it up, determined to dig deeper into the mineral rights nugget I found last night.

I didn't understand it too well, but I figured Google would explain what confused me. I started with a local property search. Then I checked some titles, but it wasn't until close to lunch time that I felt I hit pay dirt.

In a roundabout way, I'd found out about a wealthy heiress who passed away just a few weeks ago. She'd left behind no heirs and her property was subject to be snatched up by the state. But what was interesting was a nugget about the mineral rights to the property and how there'd always been suspicion over them. Apparently the woman was sitting on a gold mine of kyanite, but also diamonds. Kyanite wasn't all that expensive, but our state happened to be the number one producer of it. The diamonds, though... how in the world had that happened? How had she lived to that age with no one trying to wrest those out from under her?

Unless she'd kept it quiet all this time. To have done that, she would have had to either have very good friends or a lot of hush money.

This had to be it. I'd bet my left kidney that something in that book talked about mineral rights. I chewed on my lip. I needed to go talk to the client.

With a sigh, I poured out the now frigid coffee and rinsed my mug. I wasn't all that hungry yet. Maybe I could stop for lunch on the way to his house. I'd have to stop by the shop first to get his address. He wasn't going to be happy to see me, so I felt maybe I shouldn't call first. I didn't want him to have time to do something to the book. The odds of him not knowing about it were still decent, but this all felt too convenient for him not to. I also needed to look at my contract.

Every client I sold a rare book to had to sign my contract. I had several stipulations in it, some of them perhaps a tad paranoid, but since someone had just died, potentially over something hidden in one of those books, maybe it wasn't paranoid at all.

I kept all my documentation at the shop, so I'd have to make a quick stop there before I headed over to his house, but it shouldn't take long. I got dressed and offered to take Poppy with me, but she wouldn't get in the crate, so I left her home. It was rare that she chose to stay at the house, but I didn't mind. I worried less about her when she was here.

I tugged my sweater closer as I headed out to the car. The weather was colder than usual today, and the air felt like it had a touch of frost in it. It wasn't too late to snow here, but by now we were usually on the other side of it. I'd been wanting to plant a garden, but thought I should wait a little longer just in case.

Most of the shops around town were closed today, so I didn't see anyone when I popped into the shop. I made sure to lock the doors behind me, though, because you never knew when a customer would barge right in even without the lights on.

I hurried to the back and opened my file cabinet, flipping quickly to the records I kept on all my rare book sales. I tended to monitor those books to see where they wound up. A couple of times I was fortunate enough to buy them back at a steal, only to sell them again. Not often, but I'd made enough to pay my mortgage one month when someone I'd sold a book to had let it go for too cheap a price.

"Ah ha!" I crowed when I found the document I was looking for. Daniel Jensen was his name. I took a quick picture of the address and ran the contract through the copier before I replaced the original. His house was about thirty minutes from here. Just in case, I wrote his cell number down too.

Showing up at someone's house unannounced was the height of cringe for me. My mother would be horrified, but I couldn't risk anything happening to the book if it hadn't already happened.

I skimmed over the contract and saw the stipulation I needed. Any property hidden inside the book belonged to me even if the book was sold. Whether that would stand up in court, I had no idea, but I planned to use it to get the book back.

The drive to Candlelight Springs felt like it flew by. I stopped in at the Beans and Brew, the coffee shop I discovered when I'd last stopped in here and the same place I met Everett at. The drive through was packed, so I decided to try my luck inside. The smell of brewed coffee and fresh bread hit me as soon as I got out of my car. I inhaled and hurried in, desperate for another caffeine mix.

There were only a few people in line, so I got behind the last one, only to find the back of his head slightly familiar. I stepped to the side and peered up only to realize I stood right behind Daniel Jensen.

Small towns.

I'd wait for us both to get our coffee before I engaged him in conversation. Some things needed caffeine to begin. He spotted me right after he ordered and walked over to the waiting area. I waved at him, then rattled off my order and paid.

His eyes were just as serious as they always were. I didn't think this man was a killer. I could be wrong, but I usually had good instincts for this sort of thing. Though... thinking back to my last case, the killer was underneath my nose the entire time and I hadn't realized it until it was almost too late.

I didn't step as close as I normally would have as the thought sobered me. "Hi!" I greeted.

"Hello Ms. Adair," Daniel said. "What brings you to Candlelight Springs?"

My smile faltered. "Well, you actually."

He blinked in surprise. "Me?"

"The book I sold you. Do you still have it?"

He didn't look scared or worried or angry. Merely curious. This felt like a good sign.

"I do. Is everything okay?"

"I'm wondering if I can take a look at it?"

Daniel frowned. "That's an unorthodox request. Is there a reason?"

"I think something was left behind in it and I'm trying to locate it."

They called Daniel's name, so he stepped away for a second to get his coffee. Mine came right after so I grabbed mine as well and walked with Daniel over to a table. He motioned for me to sit.

"Elaborate," he said. He still didn't sound angry, so I kept talking.

"Have you ever heard of a man named Ricky?" I asked, blowing on the top of my latte so I wouldn't burn my tongue. I always did this and still ended up burning my tongue a good sixty percent of the time.

His eyes widened at that and immediately narrowed. "Why?" he growled. His persona changed almost immediately. I scooted back in my seat and stared at him.

"Do you know him?"

Daniel sighed. "No, but someone named Rick has been harassing me non stop ever since I bought that cursed book."

Interesting. "Is he asking to buy it back?"

He rolled his eyes. "Yes, at an astronomical amount." He speared me with his dark gaze. "Obviously there's something going on with this book I am not privy to. I'm not opposed to showing it to you, but I am the owner of it now."

I would save the contract stipulation for later. "Someone died for that book, Mr. Jensen."

Daniel's hand shook as he set his coffee down. "Excuse me?"

"A man was murdered and we suspect it had something to do with the book I sold you. He came into my shop less than half an hour before he died looking for it."

He scrubbed a hand over his face. "That's terrible."

I nodded. "This Rick person received my information illegally and found out that I was the one who had the book. Raptor Books has your information from when we first emailed each other about it, so I have no doubt they released your information to Rick as well."

"That's illegal!"

"Yes, probably so, but this is the boat we're in." I sipped on my latte. "Though I am surprised you haven't had any break-ins or further harassment."

Daniel snorted. "I have Alcatraz level security at my house."

Intrigued, I narrowed my gaze. "Why's that?"

He grinned and shook his head. "You truly have no idea who I am?"

I shrugged. "Should I?" He didn't seem familiar to me. I wasn't the kind of person up on celebrities and I rarely looked at the author picture on the back of a book. I didn't do a lot of social media, nor did I search the web too often unless I had something specific to look for.

Maybe I was a Luddite. I did watch Netflix too much, but if he wasn't on there, I didn't know who he was. I gave him an awkward grin as his eyes lit with genuine amusement.

"I wrote The Hour of our Hearts."

My mouth fell open. "No."

He nodded. "Oh yes."

I sat back in my chair, my heart beating a hundred miles an hour. I read this book last year and recommended it to everyone who came into the store. I remember specifically the book not having a photo. No one around us seemed to know who he was. "I loved that book."

"Thank you." A smile tugged at his lips.

"This is why you have so much security?"

He shrugged. "Somewhat. With the advent of the internet, people have gotten a lot more clever about finding out private things. Living here is good. Not many people know who I am and those who do, they don't spread it around. I inherited the property from my parents and my father was a paranoid man." Daniel laughed. "An IT guy. I still don't understand what it was he patented, but it made him a lot of money. So I'm surrounded by a 12 foot fence, a gate, 24-hour security, and guard dogs."

My eyebrows rose at that. "Wow." He couldn't be the murderer. I wouldn't allow it, so I decided to chance it. "I think there might be paperwork in that book for mineral rights. Someone is after it and I'm trying to track it down."

"Like oil and gas?"

"Or gems or any number of things. I don't know where the property is or what the mineral rights are for. Honestly, I'm not even sure that's what it is, but online threads suggested jewels and I can't see those being hidden in that book. I did a flip of all the pages, so if there are jewels there, I don't know how they hid them."

Daniel stood abruptly. "Grab your coffee and follow me back to the house."

"Uh." I scrambled to grab my purse and latte without spilling it and followed him out the door. "Thank you so much." This was crazy. I was going to a famous person's house. A person who wrote one of my favorite books. What a day! Harper would lose it when I told her.

Daniel wasn't kidding when he mentioned Alcatraz. He lived about twenty minutes away from the coffee shop on a mostly hidden side road. I was starting to get nervous when the road opened up and revealed a massive, sprawling estate with a massive black iron and stone gate. Daniel stopped, punched in something, and the gate swung open. I followed him in and parked in the large circular driveway in front of his house.

A stone behemoth of a mansion loomed above me. Made of light brown stone and a dark roof, it had an almost Mediterranean vibe to it. I parked behind Daniel and slowly got out of my vehicle, gaping at the house and the surrounding grounds. I couldn't tell how much land he owned, but all I could see around me was the house and carefully cultivated gardens.

"Whoa," I muttered.

Daniel came up beside me and touched my elbow. "Please, follow me."

I felt like Cinderella being escorted up to the ball. We climbed a massive staircase until we reached two large, black doors. Glancing back down at the staircase, I wondered what Daniel would do when he was old and had a bad hip. Seeing my look, Daniel chuckled. "I know. It's a lot. Fortunately, there's a door around the side, supposedly for servants." He snorted at that. "I don't have servants. Just a couple of housekeepers and someone who makes my meals once a week. I'm a hopeless cook."

He gestured for me to walk in before him and I almost stopped in my tracks when I saw the interior of his house. It looked like something out of Architectural Digest. We stood in a massive hallway. The floor was made out of a dark stone. The walls were painted in a beautiful taupe neutral, and the walls had various paintings hung everywhere. There was no rhyme or reason to it, but I found it charming, nonetheless.

"Follow me," Daniel said. "It's in the library."

I trudged behind him, my neck on a swivel as I gaped at all the sites. "Do you live here by yourself?"

"I do. I haven't quite found anyone to share it with me yet."

"Does it get lonely?" I blurted before I thought better about it.

But instead of getting offended, Daniel just laughed. "It does, but as a fellow bookworm, I'm sure you understand how wonderful being alone can be."

"I do." He was right. There was something freeing about being able to come home, kick off my shoes, and answer to no one or nothing. "No one ever tells me I read too much."

He stopped in front of a room with two French doors, his eyes crinkling at the edges with amusement. "Exactly."

I stepped into the library and halted so fast, Daniel bumped into me. "Oh! I'm so sorry. I was just surprised!"

Daniel smoothly stepped away. "It's no trouble. You're one of the first people to ever see this space. Except for my parents. This used to be my father's office, but I had it remodeled into a library. He would probably turn over in his grave if he saw it now."

"It's stunning," I breathed. And it was. Floor to ceiling shelves lined every wall and they were crammed to the brim with books. The floor was a shiny mahogany wood and Daniel had set up not one but two large, comfortable looking couches with throw pillows and blankets. Back toward the window was a large desk and a comfortable chair behind it. The desk was littered with piles and piles of paper. "Manuscripts?" I asked.

Daniel nodded. "Two. I've been working on both for far too long, but I'm hopeful I'm almost finished."

"Amazing. This room is simply amazing. May I?" I gestured to the shelves.

"Of course." His eyes glittered with amusement as I stole away from him and wandered over to the shelves. I spun when I spotted something hooked to the shelves. "A ladder?" I squeaked. "Like Beauty and the Beast?"

Daniel's rich laughter filled the room. He waved his hands. "By all means. Enjoy yourself. Explore. If you have time, I do as well."

He didn't have to tell me twice. Mr. Clark was barely in my mind anymore, I climbed to the top of the ladder, pushed off from the edge of the shelf and went flying across the room. I laughed with wild joy and reached out to grab the edge of the last shelf, bringing myself to a lurching halt. "I have to get one of these," I said to no one.

"I think your ceiling is too short in the shop, but if you get a new house, I'd be happy to give you the name of my carpenter." Daniel was bent over searching through a pile of books so he couldn't see me nod.

I perused some titles while he searched, pleased to find he had a nice mix of all genres of fiction plus memoirs, self help, thrillers, and some literary fiction. A few minutes later I climbed down, bereft at the thought of having to leave.

"We need to make a reading date," I said.

Daniel looked up from his search, a bemused expression on his face. "Oh?"

I colored. "Not a date date. Like a friend date." I pointed to the couch. "Where you can use one couch, and I use the other, and we drink wine and read. Because I love this place."

He finally pulled out the book. "That is an odd yet intriguing proposal, Ms. Adair. I'll consider it."

"Dakota, please."

Daniel nodded and headed over to the desk. He pulled out a chair for me and I pulled it up closer to where he sat. We both peered at the book. Nothing seemed out of place or odd.

"May I?" I asked.

He handed me a pair of lightweight cotton gloves. I beamed at him, pleased he was as careful with his books as I was. On that note, I looked at his windows and realized they were thick paned and darkened, so dark the books wouldn't be damaged with the light. I turned my attention back to the book and picked it up.

Carefully, I flipped through page after page, not seeing anything out of place. Daniel's dark head was close to mine. "I don't see anything," he muttered, frustration evident in his voice.

"Me neither." I peered closer and slowly started running my fingers over each page. I couldn't feel anything off or suspicious. When I finished, I pushed it over to Daniel. He put on his gloves and did the same thing.

"What exactly are we looking for?" he asked as he carefully inspected each page. He held the book up to the light and examined the spine.

"I'm not sure. I think jewels are out. Honestly, that sounded more spy movie than anything when I saw the posts about it. Maybe paper?"

I straightened abruptly. "May I?" I asked.

Daniel handed the book back over to me. I held it up and peered up at it. "Do you have an Exacto knife?"

A horrified look crossed his face. "You want to razor my five thousand dollar book?"

I shrugged and gave him a sheepish smile. "Maybe."

Daniel snorted but then realized I was serious. "Dakota. This is insane. That book was more than my first advance!"

I set the book down and peered up at him. "Seriously? The great J.D. Rosso got less than 5K for his first masterpiece? I have trouble believing it."

Daniel gawked at me before he cracked up. "Do you ever get intimidated?"

I had to laugh. "Not usually. Listen, we have the opportunity to crack a murder case if we split this book open. How do you feel about that?"

"Sounds terrible, actually. I have no desire to have my name in the news any more than it already is." He shuddered. "I feel like I bled all over that book I wrote. It was my masterpiece and sometimes I don't think I can ever top it. The less attention the better right now."

I set the book down. "You wrote a beautiful book. It came from you. No one else. The talent lies within you. Never sell yourself short. I have a plan to re-read that book once a year. Some of the passages just speak to my soul." I wiggled my eyebrows at him. "So what do you say? I'll mention my hermit friend in the press if we find anything."

"You're insufferable," Daniel muttered, but he got up to go find me a knife.

ELEVEN

Daniel had adjusted a bright ring light over our workspace. "If you're going to destroy a priceless book, at least make a straight line," he'd muttered before he handed me the knife and moved the light over top of us.

His breathing was just as erratic as mine was. I'd never destroyed a book before. This felt like the worst kind of sacrilege and if there was a book prison, surely I'd find myself rotting away there.

"Are you ready?" I asked Daniel.

"Nope." His words were short, clipped. I peered up at him and our gazes locked. I blinked and was the first to look away. Daniel was a handsome, intelligent man. And single.

And I'd just agreed to go out on a date with a handsome detective who had almost nothing in common with me except what appeared to be quite the physical attraction.

I ducked my head and steadied my breathing. "I'm not ready either," I muttered. My hand shook ever so slightly and I put the knife down and pushed the book away. "Do you have wine?"

A huff of laughter escaped Daniel. "Wine? You'd like to cut my book open while under the influence of wine?"

I nodded.

"Thank God," he muttered. "Me too. Hold on." Daniel dashed from the room and I sat there staring at the precious Hemingway volume. When I sold it to Daniel, I'd taken Harper out for a very nice steak dinner. I didn't eat a lot of steak, but there was a restaurant on the border of Silverwood Hollow and Candlelight Springs that had the best steak in the state. Harper got a filet. I got chicken and pretended not to notice Harper's horror. We split a bottle of wine and had dessert.

It cost me $300. I'd never spent that much money on a dinner in my entire life, but with Daniel's purchase of the book, I'd been flush with cash. Now, seeing the book here, those memories came flooding back. Sitting here in this library, surrounded by hundreds of precious books, what I was about to do felt like a crime.

But if it solved a murder, it needed to be done.

Daniel returned with an entire bottle of Pinot Noir and two crystal stemless glasses. His eyes were wide and his cheeks slightly flushed. "Do you feel as guilty as I do?"

he breathed as he carefully sat beside me and poured two glasses.

"Maybe worse. I'm not one to damage anything, especially not an expensive book."

Daniel waved a hand around. "My father left all this to me. I would have left it a long time ago had I not remodeled the library. It's all so ostentatious. Way too much for one person."

"Why haven't you dated anyone?" I asked. My cheeks heated and I looked down at my glass. "I'm sorry. That was none of my business."

"No offense taken." He let out a long sigh. "It isn't easy to date someone when I'm in the position I'm in. You have to fend off..." he paused as if trying to figure out how to say it. "People who are more interested in what I have than what I am."

I made a sympathetic noise. "Have you ever tried moving out of the palace and into a more normal place?"

Daniel looked aghast. "Why would I do that?"

I waved a hand. "This is all very Mrs. Havisham, Daniel."

He gaped at me. "You have some nerve."

I held up two hands in surrender. "I'm sorry but this place is enormous! Anyone would see dollar signs if you brought someone back here!"

He gave me an odd look. "Do you?"

"Well. Sure. I can tell you're rich. It's obvious. But I'm more interested in the library than your net worth. Which is why I suggested the friend dates. I really want to date your library."

Daniel shook his head and sighed. "So an apartment?" He appeared to be mulling my suggestion over.

"No. You aren't twenty. A house. A normal sized house in a normal town. You said few people know who you are, right?"

Daniel nodded.

"Then ease them into it. Slowly. Find out who they are. Find out what they like and if they're materialistic. Then for goodness' sake, sign a prenup."

"I have never met a woman like you," he muttered, and I wasn't sure if he meant it in a bad way or a good way.

I tipped back my wine. "Are you ready to do this?"

He eyed me. "It isn't me who's going to be responsible for the destruction of a priceless relic."

"I wouldn't say priceless. More like expensive. It's a Hemingway, not a Picasso."

"Depends on how much you like Hemingway, I guess," Daniel muttered.

He pulled his chair closer, so close our knees touched. I glanced at him, but he stared down at the book with a grim faced determination. "Do it," he commanded.

My lips twitched in amusement. "I used to scrap book with my Gran. It's a terrible hobby full of paper cuts and despair."

Daniel huffed a laugh. "Don't you dare make me laugh. Focus on the book and cut a straight line, please."

I hovered the knife over the book. "That's what I'm trying to tell you. I used to scrap book. I'm an ace with an Exacto knife."

I made the first cut.

Daniel's breath whooshed out.

"Shh," I urged him, my focus on keeping my hand steady. I held on to the edge of the inside front cover and carefully cut just slightly to the edge where I felt the tiniest bump. My breath cut at the first incision and sweat began to bead on my forehead.

Daniel pulled the light forward and down, angled so I could see how deep I cut. "Thanks."

"Just for the love of everything, keep it straight so I can at least repair it.

I ignored him and sliced straight down the edge of the bump. When I got to the bottom of the book, I carefully felt around the bottom edge.

There. A slight raised edge. I took another deep breath and sliced across the bottom. When I finished, I set the knife down.

"Do you think there's anything there?" Daniel breathed. He seemed just as freaked out as I was.

"I do." I carefully used the edge of my nail to lift up the edge and turned the book so the light was fully on it. A white sheet of paper gleamed back at me.

"Thank goodness," he breathed. "If you would have destroyed my Hemingway on just a hunch, I would have kicked you out of here."

I didn't have the heart to tell him that's exactly what I

did. I didn't know it was here until I saw it peeking over the edge at me. I suspected, yes. But I didn't know for sure until I saw it.

I tugged the edge of it out. The paper resisted at first but eventually slid out.

We both stared at it like it was a bug.

"You do it," Daniel said. "I can barely look at the book without wanting to scream."

I had to laugh. He was just as bad as I was when it came to classic literature and books.

I picked up the paper and slowly unfolded it. I skimmed the contents of it, my blood going cold as I read over the contents. I pushed the book back over to Daniel. "I think if you're very careful, you can repair it and no one would know the wiser. Whoever did this the first time knew what they were doing. They'd managed to carefully separate the white portion from the cardboard and had seamlessly glued it back together.

"Is it the mineral rights?"

I nodded. "I think I know why Mr. Clark died."

Daniel shut his eyes for a brief moment. "I'm so sorry."

"I may have a detective who wants to talk to you soon. Are you okay with that? He may want to set something up with Rick." I eyed the book. "Maybe we can replace that paper with something else."

Daniel frowned, his dark eyes worried, but he eventually nodded. "If he can promise to keep me out of this. I don't want my name in the news."

"I'll talk to him. If Rick wants the book so bad, maybe we can give it to him."

I held out a hand. "It was a pleasure working with you today, Daniel. Thanks for the wine."

His grip was surprisingly firm and warm. "I have to admit. This was not how I thought my day might go."

I beamed at him. "You're welcome!"

Daniel's warm chuckle followed me out of the library and into the large hall. He walked me to the door and held it open. "I don't have to think about your friend date idea. How about next Wednesday?"

I gasped. "Seriously? Can I wear pajamas?"

"As long as they're fuzzy."

"The fuzziest," I agreed. "Let's set a theme." I walked out to the porch.

Daniel tapped his chin. "How about World War Two?"

I grimaced. "That's kind of a downer."

"Seriously. Let's do Code Name Verity. Read the first ten chapters before you come over."

"Have you read it? That doesn't seem fair."

"I haven't," he said. "I've heard about it from several people. Let's start with that one and see how it goes."

"Can I bring anything? How about since we're in your library, I bring dinner? And you provide wine?"

"Fair enough, Dakota." Our gazes met and I gave him a shy smile before I bounded down the steps and back to my car. He stood at the top of them watching me and I gave him a wave before I drove away.

What a strange, wonderful day.

Daniel Jensen was nothing like I expected him to be.

And I wasn't sure how I felt about it. On one hand, I thought he could be a very good friend.

On the other, I wondered why I had no female friends except for Trudy and she'd never even visited my house.

I pondered that thought all the way home.

TWELVE

The paperwork for the mineral lights lay in my purse. I kept patting it throughout the drive home as if to reassure myself it hadn't been lost. I didn't dare risk taking this back to the shop. It needed to be kept safe. So I went to the safest place I knew.

The Silverwood Hollow Police Department was quiet today. Few cars sat in the parking lot and even fewer people milled around inside. We didn't have a lot of crime in our town, or didn't used to anyway. The past murders were unusual and anyone who committed a crime of that serious a nature usually wound up being transferred to a larger jail capable of handling them.

If Hardy was surprised to see me, he didn't show it. I knocked on the edge of the door and smiled when he saw me. "Can I come in?"

"Of course." He stood and held out a chair for me and I sank into it gratefully.

We stared at each other for a moment and the kiss we shared forced its way to the forefront of my mind. From the way he looked at me, I imagined he saw the same thing I did.

I knew the perfect way to cool our ardor. "I have something for you."

Hardy squeezed his eyes shut for a brief moment. I figured he counted to ten in his head. "Is it about Mr. Clark?"

I grinned at him. "Maybe."

He pinched the space between his brows and sighed. "What is it?" When he looked at me again, only annoyance showed in his features.

"Mineral rights."

Hardy frowned and took the paperwork. "For...?"

"Take a look. You'll see enough proof there to cast doubt on whether Mr. Clark died of a heart attack."

Hardy remained silent but unfolded the paper. I waited in silence as he perused it. When his shoulders stiffened and his lips thinned, I figure he'd seen the same thing I had. His gaze flicked to me.

"Where did you get this?"

"Does it matter?" I asked.

A muscle ticked in his jaw. "Considering this is evidence, I'd have to say yes."

"I found it in a book."

His eyebrows went up. "What book?"

"A book I sold to a client a few weeks ago."

"The same book you said Mr. Clark came in for?"

I nodded.

He tucked the paper inside of a folder on his desk. "I'll make sure it gets to the right people."

I didn't like his dismissive tone. "That's it?"

"Unless you have any more evidence, yes." He dropped his eyes to focus on whatever he was writing on.

I liked Hardy. I really did. Probably too much. But his dismissiveness riled me. Every single time.

"Are you going to do something about it?"

He dropped his pencil. "Dakota, even if we did, you wouldn't be privy to the information. You know I can't share case related information." Hardy closed his eyes and sighed. "We've been over this a hundred times."

I thought about telling him about Rick, but I decided not to. I wouldn't ask for his help again. I knew where he and I stood now, and it wasn't together. At least not when it came to casework.

"Alright." I stood. "Thank you." I turned to walk out.

I was almost out the door when Hardy said my name. Turning back to him, I waited.

"Are we still on?" There was a hopeful flicker in his eyes.

I thought about it. I really did. Dating Hardy, kissing him, they all seemed like dreams come true. But he hated this part of me. I wasn't even sure I liked it, but it was part of who I was. Every time he treated me like an annoyance rather than a peer, it felt like he'd splintered off a piece of my heart.

At my pause, something flickered in his eyes. And when I said my next words, it guttered and died.

"I think I'll pass this time, Hardy." I tapped the door frame. "Maybe next time."

I didn't wait for him to respond before I walked briskly out of the police station. It was a miracle I got to my car before the first tears fell.

THE SHOP OPENED bright and early the next morning. I'd scheduled Harper to work the first shift and I planned to come in sometime in the afternoon to do inventory. There were a few books scheduled to be delivered around three, and I liked to be there when they were dropped off so I could check them right away.

In the past, I purchased from Raptor Books, but now that they were off the table, I'd have to find a new supplier. The deliveries today were from eBay and I'd gotten them all for a steal. I just hoped the products matched the description.

I spent the last night thinking about Hardy, and Mr. Clark, and Rick, and Daniel. There were a lot of bouncing balls all around me. Hardy and I weren't dating. We never were. But it felt like I'd had a break up. I considered him my friend, but I also wanted more.

But I also deserved to be treated with respect. Though he did that on the outside, he didn't do it when he was at work. And maybe I was annoying and maybe it was annoying that he felt I got into police business too much, but I'd been instrumental in solving the cases I'd gotten involved in.

Maybe it was his ego talking.

Either way, I needed to figure this out before he and I went on any dates together.

I spent my morning researching Mr. Clark. He was married obviously, with children. They'd been involved with numerous charities. His wife was a former school-teacher until she became a stay at home mom. When her children got older, she'd gone on to form a literacy charity and remained at the helm to this day.

I couldn't find a single bad thing about them anywhere online. They didn't live too far away either, but I'd never heard of the street. An idea bloomed, so I pulled out my contract and skimmed through it until I found Mrs. Clark's phone number. When she answered, I told her who I was and asked if we could meet for lunch.

An hour later, I headed over to her house.

Mrs. Clark's home wasn't as large as Daniel's, but it was more homey. It had the feel of a place where a lot of love and laughter happened, so when she invited me in, I couldn't help but look around at all of the pictures she had hung everywhere. All of them featured either Mr. Clark or her children.

An older woman in a pair of jeans and a long sleeve shirt greeted me as Mrs. Clark led me into the kitchen. She had darker skin, black hair, and deep-set brown eyes. Her smile was bright and dimpled.

"Marta," the woman said, her language slightly accented.

"Dakota," I responded and shook her outstretched hand.

Mrs. Clark was a small woman with cool blonde hair and bright blue eyes. "Marta is an amazing chef, and I'm not sure what I'd do without her."

"Starve maybe," Marta sighed.

I let out a surprised laugh.

Mrs. Clark grinned at her. "She's funny too. Although too honest sometimes." She pulled out a barstool for me. "Please, have a seat. Would you like a glass of sangria?"

At noon? "Yes, please."

"Good," Marta said. "No important conversations should ever happen without wine. Sangria is wine lite." She poured all three of us a glass.

I looked at Marta and Mrs. Clark in question.

"She's family," Mrs. Clark said. "She knows all our secrets."

Marta waved a hand. "Do not mind me. I'll be here cooking your lunch and then I'll be out of your hair. I have another client at 3:30."

I took a sip of my sangria and almost moaned. Mrs. Clark grinned at me. "Good, right?"

"How do I get a Marta?" I said.

Both laughed. "You pay lots of money and give me free rein to experiment," Marta said.

"I can give you the second, but the first is doubtful," I responded.

Marta waved a spoon at me and went back to mixing whatever she had in her bowl.

"Mrs. Clark," I began.

"Heather," she interrupted. "Please call me Heather."

"Alright. I'd like to talk to you about Mr. Clark. I don't want to pry, but I'm interested in a few things that might help me figure out what happened."

Heather's eyes darkened in grief at the mention of her husband. "We're an open book around here. You can ask me anything."

A thought had occurred to me yesterday, something I did not want to ask, so I decided I'd wait until the end to voice it if I needed to.

"Did you or Mr. Clark have any enemies?"

Heather shook her head. "Nothing I can think of. The police asked the same thing. We had people we've made angry over the years, of course. But I can't think of a single person out of those who would want to harm my husband. We deal with a lot of people in our charities and businesses, but I can't think of anyone who has threatened to harm us."

"I'm so sorry I have to ask this."

"He wasn't cheating on me, Dakota. I'm not one of those blind to love women or anything like that. Holland was a good man. A good father. A good person. We respected each other. We loved each other. I don't believe it was anything like that."

"How long were you married?"

She smiled. "Twenty-five years. Most of them really good."

"Is there a possibility he had any other children?"

Her brow furrowed at that. "Like love children?"

I nodded. "Maybe when he was younger?"

Heather sat back in her seat. Marta's hand stopped stirring for a moment before she started back up, her movements more forceful than they'd been a minute ago.

"Well, it's something I never considered. Possibly. If he did, he either didn't know about them or he never divulged them to me. We didn't marry until he was thirty-five years old. I was 30. So maybe. I can't begin to say."

"Was he married before you?" This was something I couldn't find out online without using a paid service. That felt like too much of an intrusion, so I didn't go through with it.

"Not that I'm aware of. He never mentioned an ex-wife. We never ran into anyone claiming to be such. There were no weekend visitations or late-night phone calls or anything like that." She rubbed her eyes. "Is there a reason you're asking me all of this?"

I looked at Marta and back to Heather. "There is." I pulled out my cell phone to show her the pictures I'd snapped of the agreement.

Heather's face went white when I zoomed in. "Oh," she breathed. "Oh my."

Marta glanced at us but didn't ask. She busied herself with preparing our lunch while Heather's face went pale.

She grew quiet. "Well. That certainly changes some things, doesn't it?"

It did. Heather Clark was rich beyond her wildest dreams as long as her husband's will said she was the sole inheritor of the estate. It seemed like she would be if what she told me was true.

I reached over and patted her arm. "I'd keep that under your hat for a while. I'm going to try to find someone who was a little too interested in this."

"Where's the document?" Heather asked, her face still too pale.

"It's at the local police department. Ask for Hardy Cavanaugh if you want to see it. I'm not sure what will happen now that it's in evidence, but I'll send you these pictures if you give me your email."

Heather rattled off her email and I put it in my phone. Marta was busy dishing us up something that looked like a sweet potato mash topped with black beans and street corn. It smelled mouthwatering. She pushed our plates over without a word and started to clean up.

Something about her mannerisms seemed off. She'd been open and friendly at first, but as soon as we started talking about Holland, she clammed up. Her eyes were downcast and her lips were drawn in a thin line.

Maybe it was grief. Heather said she was like family. I watched her for a moment before Heather dug into her lunch. I followed, putting Marta out of my mind for a while.

THIRTEEN

I didn't mind eating healthy, but sometimes I equated eating healthy with food that tasted like cardboard. This was nothing like that. The sweet potato was just sweet enough to add a nice contrast to the spice in the beans and corn. I'd added a dollop of sour cream and a sprinkling of cilantro to my dish and it cooled it down just enough for it to all taste heavenly.

We ate in silence, my thoughts churning over Holland. Was it possible he had additional children angry at him? Did he have a business partner his wife hadn't known about? Why would someone kill a man who had no known enemies?

I said goodbye to Heather and Marta, who'd already started packing up to leave for her next appointment.

Heather waved goodbye from the door. "I'm cutting you a check today, Dakota."

"What? I haven't solved anything yet!" I protested.

"Darling, you've proven to me my husband was murdered. I may not know who, but you've given me some peace of mind. As bitter as it may be. It's for the full amount. If you find out who did it..." her voice trailed off. "Well, let's just say, you might have an extra Christmas this year."

Tears sprang to my eyes. "Heather, you don't have to -"

She held up a hand. "Nonsense. This is the only way I know how to thank you for bringing peace to me and my entire family." Heather waved and shut the door before I could tell her I wished I would have done it for free.

Not that she would have let me.

Harper was pouring herself a cup of coffee when I breezed into Tattered Pages. "Hey Dakota!"

"Hey Harper. Pour me one of those if you don't mind."

She brought me over a steaming mug and I inhaled the sharp scent of the brew. "Dark roast?" I inquired.

"Yup. The coffee guy brought over a bunch of new samples." Her cheeks colored prettily.

I lowered my mug. "Harper? You okay?" I grinned at her. Just recently, our coffee guy had hired some help in the form of one very handsome, very shy young man. Harper had dated a little, but her last beau hadn't worked out.

"Ben is so cute," she muttered. "Ugh. I cannot be crushing on the coffee guy. Way to make it awkward, Harper."

I laughed. "He is adorable," I admitted. "And we can get coffee anywhere. Even from Trudy. So crush away, my dear. He's smart and sweet and he recommends good beans. I approve."

Harper snorted and came around the register to plop down in the seat. "I can work over for a little while if you don't mind." She frowned. "I have a leak under my sink and I'm going to have to call the plumber out. It's going to cost a bundle."

"If you're sure." I wouldn't mind looking a little more into Raptor Books.

"Absolutely. Home ownership was way more expensive than I ever expected it to be." Harper slumped in her chair. "I sometimes wish I would have stayed in the apartment."

I nudged her with my shoulder. "It's all the initial costs. This will settle down and you'll probably end up loving it." I took a sip of coffee. "If you can hire someone to do your yard work, it gets even better. Mowing the lawn is a pain."

Harper grunted. "So what's going on with you? Anything with Mr. Clark? The entire town is buzzing about you and Hardy."

My eyebrows lifted to my hairline. "What about me and Hardy?"

"Someone overheard you giving Hardy evidence in the case." She gave me an odd look. "Then they heard you turn him down for a date."

My lips thinned. "The Silverwood Silverettes," I growled.

Harper's nose crinkled. "It's like they're everywhere.

Someone should have spotted them in the police station, though."

"They were probably bringing cookies or something just to butter someone up." I shook my head. "It's a long story. Hardy did ask me out. I said yes at first. Then I brought him evidence."

Harper winced. "Let me guess. He didn't want you getting involved and got all caveman on you."

"Yup." I kicked my feet up on the shelves below the register. "I really would like to date someone who saw me as an equal."

Her face softened. "He does, I think. I wonder if it's just hard for him to see you involved in dangerous work."

My eyes narrowed. "And it isn't hard for me? He might be too traditional for me."

"But you really like him," Harper said.

"I do." A groan slipped out of me. "I really do."

"Then tell him."

I glanced at her. "I already have."

She shook her head. "No. Tell him exactly what you told me."

"Maybe I'll just call him a caveman and see what he does."

"Careful with that, Dakota," Harper said as the bell over the door rang. "He might just throw you over his shoulder and carry you off to his lair."

And with that, I excused myself back to the office for a little while. Thinking about Hardy would result in me getting absolutely nothing done except for pining.

I couldn't find much on James Rappaport. He didn't have any social media except for Raptor Books. Their home address was listed at the same address as Raptor and his business records showed he'd opened Raptor over twenty years ago. On the surface, James held no surprises.

Catherine, on the other hand, proved a little more interesting. She was twenty years younger than James, though with the sour expression she wore all the time, it was hard to tell. She had a blog she updated regularly, but it was pretty boring and only had book news on it.

It wasn't until I stumbled across her maiden name that I struck gold. Catherine had maintained a blog from several years past about her life and how she wanted to net a wealthy man. Of course, she'd written it jokingly, but one particular blog entry caught my eye.

Written a few years prior to her marriage to James, Catherine wrote about a man named Rick and how she thought he might be her soul mate. At that, I sat straight up, goosebumps rising over my arms. I used the search feature to see if I could find his name again. Maybe in one of these posts, she had a photo of him.

I must have clicked through two hundred photos, and it wasn't until the last few that an older photo of Catherine and another man popped up. He wasn't a bad-looking guy, though there was an emptiness there that showed through even in the photos.

A knock on my office door drew my attention to Harper, who stood there with a strange expression on her face. "There's a woman here to see you. She said her name is Marta."

I blinked in surprise. "Uh, sure. Send her on in if you don't mind."

Marta walked in, her eyes wide and unsure. "If you have a moment, I'd like to talk to you."

"Of course. Please have a seat. Would you like a cup of coffee?"

She gripped her purse tight and sat down, her posture ramrod straight. "No, thank you. I won't be here long."

"How can I help?"

"Mr. Clark." She cleared her throat. "Holland. A few days before he died, a woman came to the house. She said she needed to speak with him urgently."

"A woman? Young, old?" This threw everything into chaos. Was he having an affair? Thoughts of Heather made my heart hurt.

"Youngish," Marta said. "She wasn't very friendly and refused to give me her name. Holland came out of his office and had no idea who she was. He said he'd never seen her before."

"Did you overhear what she wanted?"

Marta's fingers twisted. "Holland said she came for money and threatened to blackmail him if she didn't get it. I heard her scream that she knew he had it and that it was hers by right."

What could it be? "Did you hear anything else?"

Marta's eyes swelled with tears. "I overheard a tussle, and the woman walked out holding something. I couldn't tell what it was." She bowed her head. "He asked me not to tell Heather, even though I really wanted to. Holland said the woman wouldn't come back again."

"What did she look like?"

I grabbed a pen and wrote down the description. "Anything else you can tell me?"

"She had a man waiting for her in the car. Dark hair, but that's about all I could tell."

"Marta?"

She looked at me, her eyes red rimmed with tears. "I don't know anything else. I've never seen Holland with another woman. He and Heather were in love. I swear it. I don't know who she was and Holland said he didn't know either."

"It's very odd for her to demand money from a total stranger," I mused. "There has to be something there."

"I thought you should know. They are good people, Dakota. Please do not think ill of them."

"It's not my place to judge. Take care of yourself, Marta."

She stood, and I offered her some tissues. With a grateful smile, she headed out of the store.

Harper popped back in as soon as the bell jangled. "What in the world was that about?"

"She had some information about Holland's death. It sure seems suspicious. Someone wanted money from him right before he died."

"Do you think he was having an affair?" Harper

popped a grape in her mouth from the stash she held in her palm. "It's usually someone you know who kills you."

"Everyone in his life said no. The woman who came had a man waiting for her in the car." I glanced up at my friend. "Do you know how to do a title search?"

Harper, as it turned out, had a lot of knowledge when it came to that sort of thing since she'd just bought a house. She'd learned not to purchase anything without a title check just in case someone failed to divulge repair claims or any other number of things about the home. This, of course, made me nervous, and I was too scared to do a checked on mine when she offered. "Maybe later," I said with a cringe.

Quick to reassure me, Harper said, "Most people never have any issues!"

We pulled up the records from the clerk's office and typed in Heather's address to confirm the paperwork I'd found in the book. The rights did belong to Holland Clark, fortunately, and the clerk's office confirmed it.

However, had he not known what he was sitting on? I could only assume the reason he'd died over these were either oil, gas, or diamonds.

"Know anything about gems in the state?" I asked her.

Harper stretched at the desk. "No, but my brother has a friend who's a geologist. We can call and ask him."

I didn't know a single person who was a geologist. They always felt like unicorns. "Do you mind?"

"Not at all." Harper dialed the number and greeted the

person on the other end. "What kind of gems are famous around here?"

She glanced up at me. "Kyanite," she mouthed. I knew that one due to my own research, but I figured it was more common to find oil and gas around here than anything else. When I thought of mines, I usually thought of Arkansas. But then again, I wasn't really a gemstone kind of girl. I didn't collect crystals, and I didn't wear a lot of jewelry either.

Harper's eyes went wide. "Seriously?"

"What?" I whispered.

She waved a hand at me. "Where?" Harper went pale. "Where did you see that at?"

I was dying to know what her friend was saying on the other end of the line. Harper's hands shook. "How did that not make the news?" She squeezed her eyes shut. "Wow."

When she hung up, I almost screamed for her to tell me what happened.

"Diamonds." She said after a moment. "Found right here in Silverwood Hollow."

She didn't have to finish. "On Holland's property."

I sank back into my seat. "Holy moly."

FOURTEEN

I was just about to close up when someone came into the store. The radio was on my favorite talk show channel and the bell interrupted right as I was about to find out who the villain was. I opened my mouth to greet them until I saw who stood there.

"Catherine."

The woman stood there in front of me, her fingers tight around her purse. "I know I'm the last person you expected to see, but I just came by to apologize for what happened. James doesn't know I'm here." A weak side flitted across her face. "I must have sounded terrible when you saw me. James and I... well, we've been having some issues, and it wasn't fair for me to bring them up in front of you."

Nonplussed, I didn't say anything for a moment. "Well, that's alright I guess. It happens."

She nodded and swallowed. "I'm here because of that book."

FICTIONAL FATALITY   111

I stilled. "What about it?"

"Well, it was mine, actually. James didn't know it and he sold it. I didn't realize it was my book until it was too late."

This sounded fishy. She fell silent and the only sound was the commercial playing on the radio.

"You didn't want to sell the Hemingway?"

"It was a book that belonged to... my father. I planned to keep it for sentimental reasons."

Her father. Oh no.

The radio barked an update. *"Breaking news. Police have surrounded Raptor Books after reports of gunfire. The assailant is still on the run."*

I froze. Our gazes clashed. Catherine's eyes went cold, and she ran out of the door. In her place stepped a man I recognized.

"Ricky."

His brow furrowed at my recognition. Harper squeaked in fear, but I stood my ground. "You're in the middle of town and it's daytime. How far do you think you're going to get?"

A voice came from behind him. "Not very far."

Hardy. I slumped in relief.

"Put your hands up nice and slow and get on your knees."

Harper let out a slow breath of relief. "Talk about divine timing," she murmured.

"You have no idea." And thank goodness Hardy wasn't a man who held a grudge. If he was, I would be dead three times over.

They found Catherine down the block, still trying to run in three-inch heels. Holland never had an affair, but he did have an indiscretion in college that resulted in a daughter - Catherine Rappaport.

Rick had a rap sheet a mile long and had been seeing Catherine for the entirety of her marriage to James. He didn't know about the diamonds until just recently. Catherine apparently hung out with amateur rockhounds and had caught wind of the diamond windfall.

Trudy later told me Catherine knew Holland was her father for quite a while and was still trying to work out a way to approach him. The diamonds were just too much, so she played her hand without warming Holland up.

A DNA test was conducted later, which showed she really was his daughter. But Heather, rightly so, wanted nothing to do with her.

An autopsy and confession revealed Holland had died

from a heart attack via an induced potassium injection. Hardy was still trying to figure out the timeline of when Catherine and Rick saw him versus when the injection was given.

A massive deposit showed up in my bank account two weeks later and a dozen roses with a thank you note arrived at the store the same day the money arrived.

They say diamonds are a girl's best friend, but I'd rather have my husband back. You've done our family a great service, Dakota. Retire, go on a long trip, go back to college. Whatever you do, enjoy your life. Holland did this every day, and all I wish for is more time with him.

It was signed by Heather, Marta, and her children. I had no idea what I would do with the money. A large part of me wanted to send it back, but when I flipped the card over, there was a second note.

Don't you dare send this back. I won't accept it.

Heather and her family were sitting on a 250 million dollar diamond mine, one of the largest the country had ever seen. As soon as Catherine and Rick were arrested, Heather put the house up for sale and signed a contract to allow mining to take place. If I suspected correctly, I'd never see Heather or any of them ever again.

Hardy and I didn't speak much once the case was over, but Cole came by for the scoop. I fed him enough for a good story while keeping all the embarrassing bits about it out. We ate lunch together, and he left me sitting alone in the office.

Dusk had just fallen over Silverwood and my phone went off.

Since you had to reschedule our library friend date, I wanted to see what you thought about doing it this week? Same book. You bring dinner. I look forward to seeing you.

It was signed Library Boy. Aka Daniel Jensen.

I smiled and wrote out a response.

DAKOTA AND POPPY'S adventures continue in Paperback Perjury. Click here to order!

ALSO BY S.E. BABIN

A Shelf Indulgence Cozy Mystery Series

How about a ghost whisperer in a new magical town? Check out
The Psychic Cleaner series!

Psychic Cleaner

Like a little more magic with your cozies? Check out The
Magical Soapmaker Mysteries!

The Magical Soapmaker Mysteries

If you'd like a little more action and sass and don't mind some
PG-13 language, check out my Aphrodite series.

The Goddess Chronicles

Or, if you like a snarky bartender with a secretive mixed heritage,
meet Violet!

Cocktails in Hell

ABOUT THE AUTHOR

Sheryl is addicted to coffee and Netflix and wears her pajamas way too long to be considered proper.

She's never met a cardigan she doesn't like.

Follow her on Amazon at: https://www.amazon.com/S-E-Babin/e/B00J1J236A

www.ingramcontent.com/pod-product-compliance
Lightning Source LLC
Chambersburg PA
CBHW050418110726
47899CB00008B/2760